NEVER DIE TWICE

Iain McLaughlin

Erimem: Never Die Twice © Iain McLaughlin
Editor: Julianne Todd
Range Editor: Iain McLaughlin
First published in 2024
Erimem and associated concepts Copyright © 2024 Iain McLaughlin
All rights reserved.
Cover illustration by Dorina Petco
No part of this publication may be reproduced, stored in a retrieval system or
transmitted in any form or by any means, electronic, mechanical, photocopying,
recording or any other manner without prior written permission of the copyright
holder.
First published in 2024 by Thebes Publishing
follow us online:
www.thebespublishing.com
https://www.facebook.com/ThebesPublishing
https://twitter.com/ThebesNews
ISBN: 978-1-910868-38-6

THEBES PUBLISHING

With thanks and gratitude to the staff of Dundee's Ninewells Hospital, particularly the Renal Unit and Vascular Surgery, without whom I likely would not be here to type this.

ERIMEM

NEVER DIE TWICE

LATE SUMMER 2021

CHAPTER ONE

'Andy, I need your help – urgently.'

Andy Hansen looked up the textbook she was reading. Erimem had burst into the, thankfully quiet, canteen. She looked pretty much as nervous and worried as Andy had ever seen her. Given that they had shared countless adventures in time and space in the past few years, that was really saying something.

'What is it?' Andy asked. 'What's wrong? Aliens? Time trouble? A serial killing sociopath from the future? Again?'

Erimem shook her head and sank into a chair beside Andy. She dropped her head into her hands. 'Worse.'

Andy pushed the book aside. 'Okay, that sounds serious.' She looked nervously at her friend. 'Right, what have we got this time? What do you need me to do?'

'Hide me?' Erimem suggested. 'Break my arm? Tell me that the Drofen are preparing to invade Earth? *Anything*.'

Andy's eyebrows rose. They had been friends for several years and she could read Erimem pretty well by now. 'Something tells me that this isn't as bad as you're making out.'

'It is worse,' Erimem grumbled. '*Much* worse.'

Andy caught her friend's hand. 'Now you're scaring me. Mostly with the bad drama queen acting. Tell me what's going on.'

'Adam,' Erimem said miserably.

'What about him?' Andy blanched. She was very fond of Erimem's police officer boyfriend. Once he had accepted how impossible and often ridiculous their lives were, he had become a welcome and valued part of their little gang. 'Is he all right?'

'He is wonderful,' Erimem said honestly, 'but this... this is not good.'

'Need some info here, pal,' Andy pressed. 'What's not good?'

'There is a marriage in his family this weekend,' Erimem said glumly. 'His entire family will be there.' Her eyes dropped to the table. 'I forgot that I had agreed to go to it with him.'

'Jesus H Corbett! How could you forget that?' Andy blurted before slapping the back of Erimem's hand. 'And that's for scaring me.'

Erimem shrugged. 'We were busy. We had to save *Star Wars*, remember?'

'Oh, yeah,' Andy nodded, recalling a recent trip through time. 'We never did find out why that Jik-Jik-Harar hated the film did we? Something about one of the Cantina band being a real alien who owed him money?' Her eyes became distant for a moment. 'And I still can't believe two of those stormtroopers are you and me.'

'And then there was the famine on Venus in 2940.'

'And that malarkey at Studio 54, which we still need to finish off.' Andy waved her hands in surrender. 'Okay, we've been busy. But if you're nervous about meeting his family, why did you agree to go in the first place?'

'He cheated,' Erimem answered. 'He asked just after we had been... *affectionate*.'

Andy's cheeks puffed and she was silent for a long moment. 'Well, that's close to overshare but I did ask, I suppose.' She smiled wryly. 'At least now I know how to persuade you to do something you don't want to do.'

'But what will I do?' Erimem grumbled.

'Suck it up,' Andy advised. 'You've been a living god, the ruler of the known world, Pharaoh of the Two Kingdoms, you've led armies in battle, you've captained spaceships and you've fought single combat with a four-armed alien that had claws and swords – and you won. What is there to be scared of?'

'His mother,' Erimem answered miserably. 'What if she doesn't like me?'

Andy leaned closer and dropped an arm around her friend's shoulders. 'Well, my dear buddy, in that case you're totally fecked.'

Erimem placed her arms on the table in front of herself and her face sank onto them. 'That is not helpful, Andy. I came to you for advice because you are wise.'

'I also look great in a bikini,' Andy answered, 'but that doesn't help me give you any advice either.'

Erimem just groaned.

'Look,' Andy sighed, 'meeting a partner's parents is a big deal and it always has been.' She tried to lift her friend's spirits. 'Look on the bright side. If Adam wants you to go with him, then that means he likes you a lot.'

'I already know he does.'

'But meeting the parents is special,' Andy continued persuasively. 'It means he thinks *you* are special.'

Erimem still wasn't convinced. 'They will notice that I am different.'

Andy squeezed her friend a little tighter. 'We're *all* different, love. At least that's what the HR module I'm reading tells me I'm supposed to say.' She shrugged. 'You're just a bit more different than most… but hey, so am I. My wife used to be a pirate in the 17th Century. Helena is two and a half thousand years old and used to be immortal, Ibrahim is yer actual royalty.'

'So am I,' Erimem protested.

'Exactly!' Andy beamed. 'So we're all different, and we're all amazing.' Her words almost broke Erimem out of her fug.

Almost.

'But what if his family don't like amazing?'

Andy's shoulders slumped. 'You're impossible!'

A door opened and a tall young man somewhere in his late twenties strolled in. He wore a dark suit but his shirt collar was opened and his tie pulled loose. His short dark hair looked as if he had run his hands through it in exasperation more than once that day.

'Hey,' Detective Sergeant Adam Docherty smiled. 'Thought I'd find you two here.'

'That's why you're the great detective,' Andy answered with a comfortable smile. She liked Adam and she liked how happy he made Erimem. The relationship between a best friend and a boyfriend could be a difficult one, but Andy and Adam got along famously.

Adam put a playful frown in place. 'You making fun of me?' He glanced at Erimem. 'She making fun of me?'

Erimem smiled and shared a brief kiss with Adam as he sat with them. 'Yes,' she said. 'Andy is definitely making fun of you.'

'Thought so. I should nick you for that,' Adam grumbled.

Andy put on her best Hollywood Chicago mobster voice. 'You'll never take me alive, copper.'

'In that case I won't bother,' Adam sniffed. Can't be arsed doing the paperwork for nicking anybody anyway. Had enough of that for one day already.'

Erimem nudged Adam's arm. 'Is there a reason you are here?'

'Oh, aye there is,' Adam's Scottish accent thickened as he relaxed. 'Just wanted to make sure you're still okay for heading to Edinburgh for the wedding this weekend. I know it's a bit of a thing.'

Erimem glanced to Andy very briefly then smiled. 'I am looking forward to it.'

'She's shitting bricks about it,' Andy said lazily. 'She's been mulling hiding out in the Mutara Nebula till Monday.'

Adam's eyebrows rose. 'With Khan on the Reliant?'

Andy's knuckle rapped the table top. 'I knew you were a *Star Trek* geek. *Knew it!*'

'Guilty as charged,' Adam admitted. 'I even like the odd-numbered films.'

'He's a keeper,' Andy told Erimem seriously.

'I have no idea what you are talking about,' Erimem sighed.

'Yes, you do,' Andy answered. '*Star Trek*. Kirk and Spock.' She looked past Erimem to Adam. 'I think she needs a *Trek* marathon to refresh her memory.'

Adam nodded his agreement. 'Monday, in the villa, the big screen. Got to have "Balance of Terror" in there.'

'Good call,' Andy agreed. 'My pick is "Amok Time" though.'

'Another good one,' Adam agreed. 'Fine by me. That's two out of three. Would you go "City on the Edge of Forever" or "Mirror, Mirror" for a third one?'

'Both,' Andy decided. 'Four episodes is a better marathon than three.'

'It's a deal.'

Adam and Andy shared a fist-bump.

'Do you two actually need me here?' Erimem asked pointedly.

'Of course we do,' Andy answered glibly. 'We're just preparing your social life for Monday.'

'I am more worried about my social life this weekend,' Erimem grumbled.

Adam sighed. 'Look, you'll do great. Everybody will love you. My family aren't monsters.' He gave a brief grimace. 'Well, there *is* one uncle but he'll leave in the huff pretty quickly. He usually does. I'm not sure why he bothers to turn up, really.' He switched on his smile. 'Anyway, are you packed?'

'Yes,' Erimem fibbed unconvincingly.

Adam clearly let that slide. 'Cool. Do you prefer to fly or help the environment by taking the train?'

Erimem and Andy exchanged a near pitying look before Erimem raised her thumb and tapped the time travel ring she always wore on it. '*This* is much better for the environment.'

Adam smiled sheepishly. 'I was forgetting about that.' His knuckles rapped out a happy little tune on the table. 'Coolio. Means we can head up there earlier and spend longer with the folks.'

Erimem painted her smile on again. 'Oh, good.'

CHAPTER TWO

Rene LeVal was having a very good day.

That was not something Rene could say very often.

Once upon a time, Rene had been a hero. He was fourteen years old when Germany invaded Poland in 1939, causing France to declare war against the lunatic Hitler and his cabal of maniacs. The French had mobilised their army and taken up positions behind the defensive fortifications of the Maginot Line, ready for yet another war with Germany, and Rene was ready to fight to defend against invasion too. Unfortunately, Rene was in Belgium, unprotected by the Maginot Line and he knew that the Belgian armed forces were no match for the Nazi troops. Belgium was not at war with Germany and the politicians promised to keep it that way – but even at a young age, Rene didn't trust politicians. And, in particular, he didn't trust Hitler. Young men in Rene's local area around Antwerp quickly joined the Belgian army and not wanting to miss an adventure – and also eager to escape from his thoroughly unpleasant parents – Rene joined them. Unfortunately, the local recruiting officer had recognised him when he had tried to enlist and he had soon been dragged home by the ear by his irate mother. Her rage had been worse than anything he could imagine the Germans throwing at him.

As it transpired, Rene's inability to join the Belgian army led to him having a far more interesting war than if he had been in uniform. Germany attacked Belgium on May 10th, 1940 as part of their wider attack to the west. Belgium was taken and occupied in less than three weeks in what became known in Belgium as "the 18 Days' Campaign". Had he been in the army, Rene would likely either have been killed, captured and carted off to spend the next five years in a prisoner of war camp. At best he would have made the evacuation at Dunkerque and landed in England, unable to speak the language. There he would have spent years waiting to be sent back to liberate his homeland.

Instead, Rene joined the local Resistance movement and became a thorn in the side of the occupying German forces. He took part in blowing up rail tracks, sending troop lorries off of narrow mountain roads, killing dozens of German soldiers and he also disrupted German supply routes.

Rene was particularly fond of interfering with German supplies, which he often diverted to the cellar of a barn his family owned. Those supplies then made their way to the local villages to ensure that nobody went hungry. Of course, Rene did have to levy a small fee for his troubles. Patriotism was fine and well, but Rene wasn't going to be out of pocket for it. He discovered that patriotism and profit could go hand in hand very nicely.

Over the years of the war, Rene made himself good money and rose through the ranks of the Resistance, but his profiteering meant that nobody actually *liked* him, and when the glorious day came that Belgium was free and the Germans had been chased back to Berlin, eyes started turning towards Rene. Now aged twenty and unable to rely on the youthful looks that had got him through the early years of the war, Rene decided that his local area was too small for him and that he needed the grandeur of Brussels for someone of his stature to thrive. And so Rene abandoned his home area and his various mistresses in the local villages, two of whom were pregnant with his children, and set of for the bright lights and opportunities of the liberated Brussels.

Unfortunately for Rene he very soon discovered, like so many before him, that having been a big fish in his very little pond near

Antwerp, did not prepare him for the brutal truth of Brussels and its criminal element.

In his little village, Rene had been known as the man who had single-handedly killed a patrol of three German soldiers with his bare hands. The truth was that a stolen German bayonet and a dark alley had done most of the work but it had given Rene a reputation as a man who was to be feared. In Brussels he was nothing, and on his first week in the city he was beaten and left in the gutter twice. Penniless and destitute he had taken a lowly job for a local thug, breaking bones and giving out beatings as ordered. He had planned to move on, to build his own criminal business, to become somebody...

By the summer of 1967, Rene had gone exactly nowhere. Rene still worked for Jacques Fournee, the same gangster he had begged for work in 1945. Aged 42, Rene knew that any chance of progress in Fournee's organisation was long gone. Younger, more ambitious men got those promotions now and Rene was left dealing with the dull side of the job, picking up protection money and, if he was lucky, giving somebody a slap if they were slow to pay. The other part of his job was acting as a bodyguard to Fournee's army of prostitutes, but these days he never got to look after the young and beautiful girls and even the tired, old women who had been working since the war refused to give him any free perks of the job.

Rene's life was dismal.

Rene saw only failure every time he looked in the mirror and he didn't see how that was ever going to change.

And then an impossible piece of good fortune landed in Rene's lap.

Walking in the Rue de la Croix, on his way to collect money from Elise Boutreaux, quite possibly the most unpleasant prostitute in all of Belgium, Rene had seen a suave man who was completely out of place in that bleak part of Brussels. His suit was English, his shirt clean and crisply starched and his tie impeccably knotted. Even his leather brogues were polished until they shone. This man was either lost or he was up to no good. Given that the Rue de la Croix was part of Monsieur Fournee's territory, Rene saw the chance to do himself some good by catching this interloper operating on the boss's patch.

Remembering his Resistance training, Rene followed this stranger through a few streets, dropping back when he moved through an alley. Rene had to admit feeling pleased with himself for avoiding being detected by this man, whose twisting route through the streets clearly showed that he was up to something.

Turning out of a short street, Rene almost walked into the suited man's back, but this was not any attack from the stranger. He was staggering back as three huge men in the clothing of manual workers launched themselves into an assault on him.

The suited man was light on his feet, quickly finding his balance and he met the assault with the sort of training which screamed out that he was some kind of special services. He blocked and parried every punch or kick, with the second half of every movement being a retaliatory blow, most of which found their mark. He moved like a dervish, carefully ensuring that he kept at least one of his attackers blocked by their colleagues so that he never had to fend off all three at one time.

Those three attackers, in turn, were also trained killers. They moved with a relentless brutality, ignoring the blows landed on them. They were trained to kill, whatever the cost was to them personally. Rene knew what that meant – they weren't muscle for hire... they were government of some kind. The fact that they were dressed as they were suggested they were not Belgian.

The suited man was putting up a remarkable showing against three stronger men but eventually the numbers wore him down. One of the thugs pulled a knife and slashed at him with it, cutting his arm and on down through the jacket pocket. The injury spurred the suited man on. He caught the knife hand by the wrist, twisted, shifted his weight and sent the thug reeling into his friend. The thug backed away, shocked to see his knife embedded in his colleague's gut. He barely had time to register what had happened before the suited man's brogue slammed into his knee, bending it ninety degrees in a direction it was never meant to bend. He screamed and collapsed to the pavement.

The third thug had manoeuvred his way behind the man in the suit and gripped him in a huge bear hug. He tightened his grasp, trying to crush the wind from the suited man's body.

The man in the suit struggled. He twisted and wriggled, the tear in his suit ripping even wider, letting a small black notebook fall from the shredded pocket out onto the pavement.

Jerking his head backwards, the suited man shattered his attacker's nose, causing him to loosen his grip momentarily. He twisted hard and slammed the heel of his hand into the attacker's jaw. The thug staggered back and the suited man kicked out hard. The thug's leg skidded and he dropped to one knee. He tried to stand but he was too slow. The suited man landed a huge punch on his jaw and followed it with a hard kick to the face. The thug went limp and hit the ground hard.

The suited man looked at his three assailants and sniffed disdainfully, looking at his torn suit. 'My tailor won't be pleased,' he said in a smooth, educated voice.

His eyes settled on his torn pocket and he forced his hand inside the shredded fabric. Realising that the black book was gone, he began looking around the area desperately. He searched every inch of the vicinity thoroughly but there was no sign of the book.

A hundred yards away, Rene LeVal dipped into an alley and opened the black notebook. It took him less than a minute to realise that what he held in his hand was the most precious thing he had ever seen, that his days of reporting to Monsieur Fournee were a thing of the past and that his world was never going to be the same again.

Jacques Fournee had once been a handsome man. Being raised in poverty had made him lean, but as he had found success in the criminal underworld of Belgium and France, a taste for the finer things in life had led to Fournee gaining weight quickly. The high cheekbones on his face had soon become submerged beneath bulging jowls as excessive drinking and eating pushed him towards being morbidly corpulent. In his youth, Fournee had also exhibited an overactive libido. The prostitutes of Brussels – a pool from which he had drawn both his wife and his mistresses – had collectively breathed a sigh of relief as Fournee's increasing weight led to the death of his sex drive.

But Fournee simply substituted one voracious appetite for another.

As he lost interest in women – and indeed in men, though he had always kept that particular hunger quiet – Fournee had found his lust for sexual fulfilment turning into a desperate need for power.

Fournee owned brothels, drug dens and ran protection gangs in every major city from Amsterdam to Paris. Over the years, politicians, businessmen and notable local figures fell under his influence, at first falling for his kind and friendly overtures and then, once that "friendship" was established and good wine and beautiful women had loosened the lips of those "friends" Fournee had all the information on their lives he needed to blackmail them into doing his bidding. By 1967, Fournee had a considerable part of the political and social infrastructure of Belgium and particularly Brussels in his pocket.

It was that influence which led to Fournee finding out that a British intelligence agent was in Brussels, having recovered a notebook sold by a compromised member of the British Governments' s Cabinet to a Russian operative. That operative was now dead and the British agent was trying to escape from Brussels with the book. Russian intelligence's assassination arm had mobilised every man and woman they had in Western Europe to find and kill the British agent and to retrieve that book.

A book with every secret of British intelligence that the treacherous politician had been able gather… and a lot of their allies' secrets too. The CIA had also mobilised their European assets to get the book.

With every intelligence organisation sending their best to Brussels, Fournee had to wonder how a moron like Rene LeVal could have wound up with the book... and how LeVal could ever expect to escape from Brussels alive.

To her enormous surprise, Erimem was having rather a splendid time in Edinburgh.

She and Adam had arrived exactly where Andy had programmed their travel rings to deliver them, in a quiet, shaded corner of the garden of his parents' home in Edinburgh's well-to-do Trinity area. Adam knocked at the door at around twenty minutes to nine and a moment later watched his father's face go from surprise to delight.

'What are you doing here so early?' the older man beamed happily.

Adam looked back blankly. 'You want us to go?'

'Dinnae be daft. Come away in.' Adam's father clapped a hand affectionately on his son's shoulder and pulled him in. 'And what are you doing knocking? You've still got your key.'

Adam was playful and natural with his father. 'But I wanted to see your face when you saw us.' He stepped aside and brought Erimem forward. 'Dad, this is Erimem. Erimem, this is my Dad.'

Erimem extended her hand and shook David's. 'It is an honour to meet you.'

David's smile was warm, friendly and genuine. 'Come in, lass.'

David Docherty was an older version of his son, though slightly smaller, slightly chubbier and a good deal greyer.

The house was large and detached with a good sized garden which held mature trees and an sturdy old stone out-building which had gone from being an up-market shed to a garden room since Adam's last visit home. Clearly the Docherty family had done well for themselves and were living comfortably.

Inside, the house was brightly decorated in light colours which made the hall look far larger and more inviting.

David Docherty called over his shoulder. 'Fiona, there's somebody here to see you.'

Fiona Docherty was somewhere between fifty and sixty and still a strikingly attractive woman who would at one time have been a real beauty. Her eyes lit up when she saw her son.

'Adam!'

Adam returned the smile. 'Hi, Mum.' A moment later he was wrapped in a huge hug.

'You're early,' his mother said.

Adam managed to disentangle himself enough to breathe. 'You used to complain I was late for everything.'

His mother was still beaming. 'Did you come up by sleeper?'

'We thought we'd pick the way that got us here earliest,' Adam answered without lying or telling the truth.

Fiona Docherty's smile just got broader. 'I'm glad you did.' She turned to Erimem, aware that she had been rather rude in ignoring her guest. 'And you must be…'

'Erimem,' Adam said.

'Lovely name,' Fiona said. She sounded genuine.

'It is Egyptian,' Erimem explained.

Adam enjoyed a little chuckle. '*Very old* Egyptian.'

Erimem scowled at him. 'Not *that* old.'

Adam raised his hands in surrender.

'Well, I like it,' Fiona said. She ushered Erimem into a comfortable, brightly decorated sitting room. 'Please, come in and take a seat.'

'Have you had breakfast?' David asked. 'I'll rattle you up something if you're hungry.'

'You know what I'd kill for?' Adam said to his father. 'Proper porage. No sugar, no syrup, no cinnamon, no nothing stupid that doesn't belong on porage. Just… porage. With salt.'

'Proper porage,' his father nodded. 'My god, you've become a stereotype, laddie. You'll be wearing a kilt and saying "Hoots!" next.'

'And singing along to Jimmy Shand records,' Adam nodded. 'I am wearing the kilt tomorrow, by the way.'

'So am I,' David Docherty agreed. 'Buggered if I'm saying "Hoots!" though.'

'David!' Fiona hissed. 'Ps and Qs?' She nodded at Erimem. 'We have a guest.'

'Don't worry,' Adam said. 'Erimem has heard worse.'

'Not from you I hope,' Fiona said pointedly.

'I am in a university all day,' Erimem said. 'I hear many things worse than that, and none of them as bad as I heard from my soldiers.'

A frown crossed Fiona's face. '*Your* soldiers?'

'Erimem was in the army,' Adam explained quickly. 'An officer.'

David Docherty gave a slight bow. 'In that case I will be on my best behaviour.' I'll get started on that porage – and put the kettle on.'

Adam tapped Erimem's arm but spoke to his father. 'We'll take our stuff upstairs while you're doing that, Dad. Meet you in the kitchen in five minutes?'

David nodded agreeably. 'Take your time,' he said. 'I haven't had coffee yet this morning so I'm still a bit slow.'

'We've put Erimem in the spare room,' Fiona said.

Adam's eyebrows rose.

His mother kept a straight face for just long enough, before it cracked. 'Don't be daft. Your room's exactly as you left it – just a bit tidier.'

That was roughly the moment Erimem knew she was going to enjoy the company of Adam's parents.

'Good,' Adam said, giving his mother a look which somehow managed to still be affectionate as he glared daggers at her.

'Besides, we don't have a spare room these days,' Fiona continued. 'That fourth bedroom is your father's study now.'

'I always wanted a study,' David said to his son. 'Of course, now I'm retired I don't actually have anything to study in my study but... well, there we go.'

Adam sighed. 'Well, you're both as mad as you were when I ran away to London – thank god. See you in five minutes.

Picking up their luggage, Adam led Erimem upstairs.

Andy Hansen was settling down to a very quiet, very relaxing weekend. Her rather fabulous wife Olivia was out shopping, Ibrahim was back in Egypt for a really dull conference he hadn't been able to talk his way out of, and of course Erimem and Adam were in Edinburgh at a wedding. Ibrahim's wife Helena was still around – she had managed to avoid the Egypt trip and the risk of meeting her in-laws. The simple fact was that Helena did not meet with the approval of Ibrahim's family and neither of them cared. Making herself unavailable due to work commitments had been a shrewd move. Andy and Helena would probably have a coffee at some point that day and catch up, and quite possibly watch *Strictly* together to ridicule the judges' scoring. Other than that, it was going to be a relaxing day.

Andy felt suddenly sick.

Something in her stomach lurched and her head reeled dizzily.

She wasn't in her kitchen anymore.

The swish, gleaming worktops and modern appliances were gone. Instead, she was in ancient Alexandria, sitting on the edge of the harbour next to a hook-nosed old man with twinkling eyes. Their feet dangled as if they were children.

'Okay,' Andy said. 'What gives? Why am I here and who are you? I've got more questions. I'll put them in order while you answer those three.'

The old man's eyes sparkled with amusement. 'Will you?'

That was all he had to say for Andy to know exactly who she was speaking to. Erimem has discussed her mystical time-defying grandfather and his habit of dragging her into dreams and visions many times. Andy had no doubt that this old codger was Erimem's grandfather. 'Hang on,' she said. 'You wouldn't happen to be the old pharaoh, would you?'

The old man sniffed with just a bit too much disdain at her description for his annoyance to be anything but a performance. 'That's not a dignified way to talk about the ruler of the known world and the father of Egypt.'

'Oh god,' Andy muttered sourly. 'She's right, you really *are* annoying.'

'I know.' The old man gave a happy, almost toothless grin.

Andy decided it was time to put her foot down – a sandaled foot she noted, wondering what had happened to her trainers – and take control of this latest trip to Wacko-land. 'Look, hate to tell you this, but your aim is off,' she said firmly. 'Assuming you *are* Erimem's spooky-wooky-woo-woo space-grandad, you're supposed to be in *her* brain, not mine.'

The old fellow was not perturbed at all. 'This is an experiment,' he explained casually. 'Should I ever have trouble contacting my grand-daughter, I need to know I can reach someone else's mind.' He sniffed, pleased with the explanation. 'By the way, you are going to have a terrible headache after this.'

'If I do you're going to have terrible bollock-ache,' Andy snapped sharply.

That just made the old pharaoh laugh. 'I can see why Erimem likes you,' he cackled. 'You're annoying as well.'

Andy pulled her scowl even lower. 'Thanks a bundle,' she grumbled. She had a feeling things were getting decidedly off-topic. 'Look, I don't want to say this hasn't been a blast – even though it hasn't – but if you don't mind, I've got a comfy sofa and a load of lazing about to get on with.'

'You should make coffee for Helena,' the old man said. 'She will be at your home in a few minutes.'

'Might do,' Andy grumped.

The old fellow's mouth widened into a crafty smile. 'And when you are having coffee, you can tell her the task I have set both of you.'

Andy puffed her cheeks out and blew hard. 'Oh, bugger.'

Erimem's morning was proving to be a delight.

She hadn't known what to expect from Adam's bedroom. Part of her expected it to be the sort of sweaty cave Andy's brother Matt had turned his bedroom into, but instead Adam's bedroom was bright and airy, wallpapered in a pale blue and white pattern.

He had bookcases on which a few old photographs were perched. It wasn't the boy's room she had thought it might be. Adam had already been a grown man when he had left.

After unpacking the clothes that needed unpacked and hung up – particularly Erimem's dress and Adam's kilt for the wedding – they headed downstairs and found Adam's parents in the kitchen, laughing and talking together as they made breakfast.

Erimem accepted toast and orange juice while Adam looked delighted by the bowl of real porage placed in front of him by his father.

'Thanks, Dad.'

Fiona Docherty scowled as her husband placed a platter of bacon, eggs and sausages in the middle of the table. 'What did your doctor tell you?'

The eggs are poached, the bacon and sausages have been through the George Foreman,' David answered. 'I do listen to what he tells me and I take the healthy option.' He shrugged. 'Sometimes.'

'You are impossible.' Fiona shook her head but she held the plate out towards Erimem. 'Do me a favour, dear, and put some of this out of temptation's way.'

Adam chewed quickly at a mouthful of porage and swallowed it down. 'Are those sausages from Wullie Allardyce's shop?' He looked across at Erimem. 'Wullie's the best butcher in Edinburgh. He told me his dad, Lamont, came up with the recipe for those.'

'That's true,' David agreed with his son. 'Best black pudding as well.'

'You're not allowed that either,' Fiona said nonchalantly.

David wrinkled his nose and scowled at her.

'You'd be doing yourself a favour if you tried those sausages,' Adam said sagely. 'In fact, I might snaffle some of that myself. Especially if they're your own eggs, Dad.'

David saw the frown appear on Erimem's face. 'He doesn't mean that I lay them myself.'

'I would hope not,' Erimem answered innocently. 'That would *really* sting.'

'He has an allotment,' Fiona explained. 'He keeps chickens there.'

'Ah,' Erimem nodded her understanding. 'It is wise to keep them away from the house. Birds can be annoyingly noisy.'

'Exactly what I said,' Fiona agreed.

David just grimaced theatrically. 'You don't like my chickens but you like their eggs.'

Fiona replied without missing a beat. 'I like bacon but I wouldn't have pigs in the house.'

It was obviously a discussion they'd had often enough for it to become a joke because they both laughed at it.

'Do you keep animals yourself, Erimem?' Fiona asked.

Adam bit down on a smirk. Erimem had a herd of semi-sentient holographic woolly mammoths living in the grounds of her villa... which was accessed through a cupboard door in her house... and he wasn't sure if the villa really existed or not.

Erimem obviously saw his doubts and answered, 'Not really, no, but I am very fond of animals.'

'I thought you might have kept chickens or birds the way you talked about them,' David said.

Erimem shook her head. 'No, my father kept peacocks and horses and...' she stopped. Explaining the extent of a pharaoh's menagerie was probably not a good way to introduce herself to Adam's parents. 'My father also liked animals.'

The use of the past tense regarding Erimem's father was a red flag that the conversation could turn maudlin if that topic was pursued, so Fiona parked it momentarily and moved on. 'Do you have any plans for today?' she asked.

'Travelled four hundred miles,' Adam answered, 'so I thought we might spend some time with my parents, even if they are knocking on a bit.'

David Docherty buttered a slice of toast. 'Any more talk like that and you definitely won't make it to this age.'

Adam just laughed, and Erimem couldn't help joining in. She liked the comfortable, easy relationship Adam had with his parents. It was completely different from the rigidly structured and formal relationships she had set out for her with her mother and more particularly her father.

'We're heading into the centre in a bit,' Fiona said. 'I need to pick up a few things for tomorrow. If you want to join us we can have lunch in town.'

Adam nudged his father. 'We could do Rose Street.'

Edinburgh's Rose Street had once been famed as a sort of endurance course for boozers and tourists out for a hard drinking session. It had seemed that every other doorway led into a new pub and the test was to see how far along the street a boozer could get before succumbing to their partying. Whether the rumours about Rose Street were true or if they had simply been exaggerated over the years, nobody was quite sure but it led to the place being legendary in the city.

'It's not what it was,' David said sadly. 'It's a bit posher these days.'

'He means you can buy food there,' Fiona smirked.

Adam looked to Erimem. 'What do you think?'

She nodded. 'I think I would like to see your city.'

The old pharaoh had not been joking. Andy had a skull-splitter of a headache and she had resolutely decided that she was indeed going to boot his bollocks in if she ever saw him again.

Helena found Andy sitting at the island in her kitchen, head in hands, looking like she was at death's door.

'What's the matter with you?' Helena asked. 'A few drinkies too many last night?' She sounded quite sympathetic. Or jealous. Andy couldn't be sure which.

'Neither,' She answered sullenly. 'I just got a psychic visit from Erimem's weirdo grandad.'

Helena's eyes widened. 'His aim was off, wasn't it?' She began to give Andy a quick examination, peering at her eyes and checking her pulse.

'Nope,' Andy answered. She explained her meeting with the pharaoh – and made a point of reiterating quite how annoying the old codger was.

'So what did he want you to do?' Helena asked. 'I think you'll be fine, by the way.

'Us,' Andy corrected her. 'Thanks for the all clear but it's what he wanted *us* to do.'

Helena's voice went flat. 'Where did the "us" come from, pal?'

'Asked for you explicitly,' Andy said.

'I don't think I like the sound of that.'

'I'm bloody sure you won't like the sound of it,' Andy answered.

Helena waited then pressed at Andy to continue. 'Well?'

Andy sighed. 'How well do you remember 1967?'

Helena's mouth quirked a bit. 'I may be the only one who was there that can say this, but I remember it pretty well.'

'Good,' Andy said, reaching for the box of paracetamol on the work surface, 'because that's where we're going.'

The Assassin arrived on mainland Europe by stepping off of a routine late afternoon flight from London at Amsterdam's newly expanded Schiphol Airport. A mousy brown wig, heavy glasses and an unfortunate-looking but carefully created set of false teeth changed her appearance completely. When added to her padded, frumpy clothes the whole effect added twenty years to her while ensuring that no-one would give this unremarkable middle-aged woman a second look.

That was exactly what she wanted.

The Assassin had gone by many names and in the concealed compartment at the bottom of her suitcase she carried half a dozen passports from various countries, each under a different name and nationality. She entered the Netherlands under a Norwegian passport calling herself Alicia Huberman. She had intended to follow her prepared plan of making her way to a safe house where she would, remove her disguise and get rid of these terrible clothes, and then leave her luggage, picking up the replacement set that she had arranged to have ready for her, and then move on to Amsterdam Centraal Station, where she would travel as Swedish teacher Ilsa Lund to Brussels in Belgium. The journey of 176km would only take a few hours and she would find her weapons waiting for her in their specially designed suitcase when she arrived in Room 17 of her chosen hotel, *La Liberte*. She would never admit to anything as weak as having a favourite hotel, but she found *La Liberte* to have everything she needed, from excellent multiple exits, access to the sewers in case of emergency, and most of all, a staff she could bribe, blackmail and control.

However, while still in Schiphol, the woman still in the persona of Alicia Huberman saw another passenger from her flight just ahead. He was just heading into middle age and wore a suit that had never quite been in style. Over it he wore a raincoat which looked as if he hadn't taken it off in days. His brown Trilby was tilted forward as though he was keen to keep the sun out of his eyes. That did not surprise her. She imagined that he had flown from New York to London and then immediately caught the next flight to Amsterdam. It wasn't a surprise that he looked tired. She had never encountered the man before but she had read his file several times while still employed by her own country's secret service. That was before she had staged her own death and gone into business as a freelancer. The man ahead had looked younger in his file photographs. The three years since then had obviously been hard for him but he was still undeniably Martin Baines, the agent the CIA chose for its most important cases in Europe. He had over a dozen confirmed kills to his name and more than double that number were unconfirmed but attributed to him. He was reputed to be ruthless and brutal. He was unmarried, had no known vices, and neither drank nor showed any interest in women. Or indeed in men, for that matter. His sexual preferences only interested the Assassin if they could be used as a weapon. Baines was known to smoke, but not to excess with his cigarette consumption estimated at between five and ten a day.

Baines' presence put the Assassin on alert. She had known that there would be competition on this job, and that she would probably have to eliminate some of them.

She hadn't expected someone like Baines, though.

Baines was elite, he was prestigious.

Baines was a prize.

Killing Baines risked bringing the sort of official attention that people in her line of work tried hard to avoid, but it also brought them to the attention of people who could give her the most exclusive jobs... the best paying jobs. Two or three of those major engagements would set her up for life, and the Assassin had been very careful to keep her tracks covered. She had made sure that nobody knew who she was or where she lived. She enjoyed her quiet life in the Scandinavian countryside, only occasionally visiting the local towns and villages to shop or take a lover when the mood was upon her, but those entanglements never lasted. She made sure of that. A few really big, well-paid jobs and she could retire in comfort to that life for the rest of her days.

She followed Baines at a distance of about ten yards, blending into the crowd, keeping her eyes down as much as possible. Within a dozen steps, she knew that he was heading to the same part of the airport she would have been going to anyway. He was catching the connecting coach to the train station. Normally his agency would have had one of their agents in the city pick Baines up and drive her to Centraal but Baines was too sharp for that. If a CIA car was spotted by any of the opposition agents, Baines' presence might be blown before he could even leave Amsterdam. He was keeping his presence low-key. It was sheer luck that she had spotted him.

It was a piece of luck she intended to capitalise on.

In the end, killing the CIA's most feted agent was surprisingly and disappointingly easy.

Baines took a seat three from the back of the coach and carefully watched every passenger who moved closer to the back of the bus. He saw the Assassin – except that he didn't see her at all. He saw a mousy woman with bad teeth and poor eyesight and he dismissed her.

At that moment, the Assassin knew she was going to take great pleasure in killing this man.

She wasn't sure if he had dismissed her because she looked middle aged or because she had thick glasses or because she didn't look pretty enough to pay attention to. More likely he disregarded her as a threat for all of those and the largest reason of all – she was a woman.

He wouldn't be the first she had killed because of that error in judgement, and he probably wouldn't be the last but it might just be the most enjoyable kill of them all.

She took the seat behind Baines and sat quietly, turning her head to look out of the window at the bustling crowds coming to and from the airport, living their dull, pedestrian little lives, working themselves into oblivion in the hope that they might escape to the coast for a few days every year.

While her face remained neutral and impassive, everything inside her being sneered at these people. They were pathetic.

She relaxed in her seat, ignoring the irritating, balding man who sat beside her. He tried to engage her in conversation but she feigned not understanding his language and went back to staring out of the window.

The trip to the train station would take between twenty and forty minutes, depending on the traffic. If Baines followed CIA protocol, when the coach reached the station he would be the last passenger off, having made sure that everyone else getting off was no threat and then he would make his way to his train.

That all suited the Assassin just fine.

Amsterdam was a beautiful city. She took in the architecture, the trees, the history... she absorbed it all as the coach made steady progress towards Centraal. But for all that time, while she watched the city, part of her attention remained on the slightly out of focus reflection in the window of the side of Baines' face in the seat ahead. He didn't just look tired. He looked weary through to his bones. That was when she understood where he was in his life. He had reached the point that many agents eventually got to. He had seen enough, done enough, experienced enough and he didn't want to do the job anymore. She had seen that expression so many times on so many faces. Maybe that was why he had missed her as a threat.

The coach finally reached Centraal and the passengers began to file off. Baines and the Assassin were the last rise, letting everyone else make their way off the bus ahead of them.

Baines gave her a joyless, overly polite smile and indicated that she could go first. She replied with a courteous nod and as he put his hand on the back of the seat to move more steadily she brought her hand down on top of his quite gently.

'Thank you,' she said.

His eyes widened as he felt the sting of the needle hidden in the large costume ring she wore on her hand. He opened his mouth to speak but the toxin from the ring was already in his system. He was already having difficulty controlling his actions. The poison would start burning him within a few more seconds and then there would be numbness. Within thirty seconds it would all be over.

Baines dropped backwards into his seat.

When he died thirty five seconds later, the Assassin was already off the coach and in a taxi heading away from the station.

By the time Baines' body was found, the Assassin had already visited her safe house and changed her appearance. The ambulance was still by the parked coach as her taxi dropped the Assassin, now travelling as the younger and more glamorous Ilsa Lund with her Swedish passport.

She barely gave the ambulance a second glance.

'You and I are not going to be fashionable in 1967,' Helena said thoughtfully.

She and Andy were inside Erimem's habitat, having dressed in clothes appropriate for the era they would be travelling to. They had both looked fabulous in mini dresses but had eventually given way to practicality and chosen narrow trousers and patterned tops. Andy's was a long sleeved t-shirt with a spiral design while Helena wore a pink blouse patterned with large blue and yellow flowers.

Andy didn't follow her friend's concerns. 'How do you mean?' she asked. 'We can rock any outfits.'

Helena poked at her own chest. 'Anything over a B cup and you're not in fashion,' she said ruefully. 'I remember moaning to Mary Quant about that.'

Andy sniffed and pointed a finger at the floor. 'It's down there.'

Helena frowned in confusion. 'What is?'

'The name you dropped,' Andy answered with a grin.

Helena waved the accusation away. 'Oh, that's nothing,' she said nonchalantly. 'I spent most of '67 hanging with Jane and the boys.'

Andy adjusted her finger so that it now pointed at her own face. 'Blank face here?'

'Jane Asher and the Beatles,' Helena explained. 'Jane was engaged to Paul. God, she was in bits when they broke up.' Her memory drifted back more than fifty years. 'We drank a lake of wine to get her over all of that...' She frowned and shrugged. 'But that was '68, not '67.'

Andy always loved it when Helena dropped little bits about her past. 'So in 1967 you are Miss Party-Pants with the Beatles?'

'Pretty much,' Helena agreed. 'Sergeant Pepper was finished and came out in '67 – I'm on it you know,' she added nonchalantly. 'One of the voices in a fade out – and the album was a bit of a hit, probably because of me, then they started work on the White Album.' An odd wistful sile spread across her face. 'George was gorgeous, you know. Totally platonic, no shenanigans, but he was gorgeous. And so sweet. Well, they all were. Not like the Stones. They were wild.'

Andy coughed meaningfully. 'Think we're off-topic here,' she said. 'We were discussing that we're unfashionable for being more Barbara Windsor than Twiggy in the bazooms department?'

'So we were.' Helena sighed and put her memories back in the past. 'And, yes we are too chesty to be fashionable in 1967.' She glowered at her chest. 'Damned annoying things.'

'They absolutely are,' Andy agreed, leading the way into the little side room which held the controls of the machinery which could send them anywhere in space and time. She picked up one of the time travel rings and slipped it onto her right hand. 'But we'd better get groovy, baby.'

Helena scowled at her friend. 'Don't do that,' she said, putting a ring on her own finger. 'We didn't talk like that… not often anyway.'

Andy operated the controls and they stepped onto the little travel area. 'You're no fun anymore,' she grumbled, teasing her friend.

Helena's caustic reply was drowned out by the spitting ball of lightning that carried them away to the past.

CHAPTER THREE

Erimem was falling in love with Edinburgh.

The old city had thrown off her grey morning blanket of cloud and was now basking under clear blue skies. Even the chill breeze which often blew up the Forth from the North Sea, was on its best behaviour and was keeping its distance. The city was busy, with lots of people wandering the streets and going into shops. A good number of people – particularly among the younger population – still wore masks when they were out and about and there was a fair bit of social distancing still happening in shops but there was a hint of normality returning.

She liked the Victorian gothic Scott Monument which stood on Princes Street. It was of a different style to the giant monuments at home in Egypt but it was imposing and had scale. If she liked the Scott Monument she *loved* Edinburgh Castle, standing high over the city on Castle Rock, watching over the capital like an eternal guardian. Edinburgh was nothing like her beloved Thebes but she felt comfortable there; she felt at home.

While all four of them had gone shopping, the party had more than once split in two with Adam and his father occasionally disappearing for five minutes here and there while Erimem tended to stay with Fiona.

'Don't worry about Adam and his dad wandering away,' Fiona said looking into the tartan festooned window of a tourist shop and wrinkling her nose in distaste. 'They've been doing that since Adam was a wee laddie.'

'I know what that means,' Erimem said happily. 'It means "small boy".'

'Teaching you the lingo, is he?' Fiona chuckled approvingly. 'Just make sure he learns Egyptian in return. It's only fair.'

'I will suggest that,' Erimem agreed.

They moved on, peering into various shop windows before wandering into a tourist gift shop.

'Why are we in here?' Erimem asked.

'I'm going to buy a few really tacky knickknacks,' Fiona explained. 'My sister hates them, so I'm getting some for her. I'll give her them at the wedding tomorrow.' Erimem's eyes widened in confusion. 'We don't get on,' Fiona went on. 'Me and my sister. We're not close. I like to annoy the hell out of her.'

Erimem couldn't help but smile. 'Siblings can be... difficult.'

Fiona's eyes fell on the soft toy of a stereotypical Scotsman with red hair and beard, kilt and Tam o' Shanter. It was magnificently awful. 'She'll hate this,' she said, lifting the toy.

Erimem followed suit and also picked up one of the toys.

'You got a sister you want to annoy as well?' Fiona asked.

'A friend,' Erimem answered. 'I do not have any siblings anymore.'

The "anymore" caught Fiona's attention. 'Oh, I'm sorry, dear. I didn't mean to pry.'

Erimem had long ago accepted the death of her brothers. She still felt their loss, but she rarely allowed it to become oppressive. She had even found a way to use time travel to find her own way to say goodbye to Mentu, the brother she had been closest to.

'They died a long time ago,' she said evenly, 'but I will make sure they are never forgotten.' Her nose wrinkled as a memory from her childhood flickered through her thought. 'Even if they were *very* annoying.'

Fiona dropped an arm on Erimem's shoulders and gave her a friendly, motherly squeeze. 'Siblings can be, can't they?

Anyway,' she said, taking a livelier tone, 'I won't pry any further.'

Erimem took the cue and also returned to the lighter atmosphere they had enjoyed. 'Thank you. Tell me,' she said, looking round the shop, 'is there anything here that would really annoy Adam but he would feel that he *had* to put on display because it was a gift from me?'

'Almost everything,' Fiona nodded. 'He hates this teuchter stuff.'

'Teuchter?'

Fiona shook her head. 'I'll let Adam explain that to you.'

'As long as it annoys him,' Erimem agreed impishly.

'I can see why you and Adam get on.' Fiona said approvingly. 'You're full of mischief, aren't you?'

'I try to be,' Erimem admitted. 'Is that a bad thing?'

Fiona waved off the younger woman's concerns. 'Not even a wee bit. Mischief keeps things interesting.' She offered a secretive little glance at Erimem. 'I still wind up David all the time. He does the same to me. It's good fun.'

'This explains a great deal about Adam,' Erimem said slowly. 'He is also full of mischief.' She returned the smile. 'And I like that.'

'Good.' Fiona turned her attention back to the shop. 'Now, what other tourist tat can we get to annoy people with?'

As usual when he returned to Edinburgh, Adam had made his way to his favourite bakery.

And as usual his father had joined him. 'You said your lass was army?' David Docherty asked.

Adam wasn't sure how Erimem would react to being called "his lass" but he didn't object to it. He just agreed. 'Yep.'

'What rank?' David asked curiously, picking up two packets of his son's favourite Empire biscuits.

There was no mystery about why the older man would be interested. He had been in the army himself. Of course, a completely honest answer might have made David's head explode, so Adam gave an honest reply, albeit couched as a joke.

'Well, if you ask her, she ran the whole army herself.'

David chuckled. 'Definitely an officer, then.' He didn't sound as if he held that against her. 'Did she see combat?'

For the first time, Adam wondered if bringing Erimem home was a mistake. He didn't like misleading his parents. On the other hand, he couldn't exactly tell them the whole truth.

He stuck to being honest but paring it back to the minimum. 'A lot,' he said, 'but she doesn't talk about it much.' He asked for half a dozen sausage rolls.

David nodded. 'Probably means she saw a lot of bad stuff.'

'She did,' Adam answered.

David ordered a couple of Forfar bridies, then thought for a moment before he nodded and sniffed. 'Well, we'll not mention it,' he said.

Adam slapped his father's shoulder appreciatively. 'Thanks, Dad.'

Adam paid for their order and they wandered back out into the sunlight.

'You like her?' David asked.

'I wouldn't have brought her if I didn't like her,' Adam answered.

He hadn't answered the question and they both knew it.

'Ye ken fine what I mean,' David pressed. 'You *like* her?'

Adam Docherty loved his life in London. He loved his job with the police there and adored everything about his unlikely new secret life, too – but he really missed being able to talk with his father this way.

'Aye,' he said firmly. 'I do.'

That definitely seemed to please David. 'Should we get used to seeing her?'

In honesty, Adam hadn't thought too much about the future. There had never been time. Oddly, time travel meant he was usually short of time. But the answer here was instinctive. 'I really hope so.'

'Good,' David confirmed his approval, 'she seems like a nice lass. Now, let's find her before your mother scares her off.'

Andy and Helena had arrived in Brussels – and Andy was not even slightly surprised to find out that her friend knew the city well. Having lived as long as she had, it seemed that Helena had visited everywhere at least twice. It took her a moment to get her bearings, but she was soon confidently leading the way through the city.

Andy followed closely behind her fried. 'You know where we're going?'

Helena paused and looked around again. Things had obviously changed since she was last in the city… whenever that might have been. 'Yep. I miss Google Maps though.'

With a guilty look, Andy held up her mobile phone. 'Um… I brought Google Maps. Did a bit of borderline genius jiggery-pokery so we can use it anywhere.'

'That's thing's an anachronism!' Helena waved for Andy to put the phone away. 'If anybody got hold of that tech the changes to the timeline would be catastrophic.'

Andy gave a slightly embarrassed grin. 'If anybody got hold of the phone and saw the pics on it, that would be catastrophic, too.' She shoved the phone back in her pocket. 'So nobody's getting it.'

'Yep. Getting that out of sight is a good idea,' Helena said. 'Oh, and thanks for the overshare about you and Olivia's photographic habits.'

'We're an old married couple,' Andy protested. 'We can be as disgraceful as we want.'

Helena took another look around and frowned. 'I might need those maps. A city really can change a lot in seventy-odd years.'

'At least we're not likely to run into any of your old cronies.'

Helena had finally found her bearings. 'This way, I think,' she said, leading Andy across the street.

'You *think*?' Andy asked.

Helena frowned in reply. 'Don't pressure me. I'm old.'

Andy offered a placating smile. 'You don't look a day over two thousand.'

Helena's nose wrinkled appreciatively. 'Aw, thanks. You say the nicest things. This way.'

Rene LeVal knew that he was in trouble.

He lived in dreadful little flat in one of Brussels' less agreeable neighbourhoods, supplied by Monsieur Fournee. The boss liked to keep his lackeys close to the people they terrorised. It was good to keep a physical presence among the masses as a reminder.

Rene LeVal's flat was on the top floor of an old building that might once have been quite attractive but, as Rene often pointed out, like the prostitutes working in the brothel on the first and second floors, time had not been kind to the building.

The flat contained a small living room with a tiny kitchen area, a pokey little bedroom and a bathroom which had walls blackening with mould. On a good day it could be called a hovel, but it was the only home Rene had, and it was where he kept the meagre possessions he had gathered over his twenty years in the city.

Despite his lack of success, Rene was not a stupid man. He was good at the job he did, and he had developed an instinct for when trouble was brewing. Even before he had entered the miserable little outer door covered with grime and flaking bottle green paint, and started his way up the stairs, Rene knew that his flat was being watched. There were two men in doorways opposite, the opium den and the strip club. Their clothes were too clean and tidy to be either locals or customers of those establishments. Not only that, their eyes were carefully trained on Rene's front door rather than the drugs or the women a customer would have come to sample.

At most Rene would have fifteen minutes before Fournee's men kicked in his flat's door. He didn't know what Fournee's involvement with the suited Englishman was and he didn't know how Fournee had got word that Rene had the notebook but what mattered was that Rene hadn't taken it straight to the boss. That would mean only one thing to Monsieur Fournee – Rene was going into business for himself.

And on that matter, Fournee would be correct. On his way back to his flat, Rene had stopped at the *Café Mistral* and a telephoned a man known as Le Balance... the Scales. He was one of three brokers in Belgium who could get Rene the money he knew this notebook was worth, and he was the only one of the three Rene had ever had any dealings with.

Unsurprisingly, Le Balance knew of the book and had, in fact, been willing to cut a deal for it with the three Russians Rene had encountered earlier, if they had been willing to betray the Kremlin. The broker was now ready to offer Rene that very same deal – and as a bonus arrange safe passage out of Belgium.

Rene quickly changed into his newest and smartest clothes, and gathered all of the money he had saved from the various hiding places he had around the flat. He pocketed his trusty flick-knife and the Luger pistol he had taken from a German officer he had killed during the war. The pistol was old but it worked, and the distinctive shape was a frightening callback to those terrible but profitable days in the Resistance.

Closing the door, Rene hurried downstairs, past a door from which he heard a man's animal gruntings and the artificial squeals of simulated pleasure from his companion. He guessed Elise wasn't having a good time, but at least it wouldn't last long.

Once on the ground floor, Rene kept going down the stairs, into the basement. Rene was many things but he was not stupid enough to use the front entrance to leave when he knew it was being watched. Chances were that the back exit was being observed too. There was, however, a third way out. It dated back to the war. The basements of all of these houses in the street had been adapted slightly with holes in the basement walls, so that they could flee from once house to the next without ever stepping foot outside. Rene had found out about the escape route when a philandering husband from three doors along had escaped his angry, kitchen-knife wielding wife through them... though Rene did wonder if the man was a fool for choosing to escape to a brothel after being caught with another woman.

Quietly and efficiently, Rene made his way to the furthest building in the street, carefully heading up the stairs without being seen, and then slowly emerging from the door and losing himself in the crowds on the street.

He used public transport to reach *L'Hotel du Presidente*, one of Brussels' most expensive and exclusive hotels. He did not go to Reception to have them call up to Le Balance's suite. His host would not appreciate any of his guests advertising their arrival in that way. Instead, he made his way to the lift and went up to the sixth floor. A tall mountain of muscle was waiting. He looked as if his biggest daily task would be making sure he didn't burst out of whatever he was wearing. The suit he was squeezed into was had not been designed for his kind of muscles. He had long sandy hair and a bushy moustache of the same colour. In a Dutch accent he introduced himself as Piet.

Rene gave the password he had been instructed to use by Le Balance.

Piet nodded and led the way along the corridor. 'This way.' They passed two more suited musclemen who were standing guard a few steps out from the door to the suite at the end of the corridor. Piet knocked at the door and waited for the response of "Come in" before opening the door and ushering Rene in.

Le Balance was a man of average height but a rather slight build. His tailored suit was Italian cut and his shoes were handmade in Milan. His hair was carefully cut and styled rather shorter than was the latest fashion. His dark eyes were heavily lidded but they took in everything and there was an obvious cunning in them. In his hand he held a cut crystal glass filled with an undoubtedly expensive whisky. He met Rene with an insincere smile.

'Monsieur LeVal,' he said in a cultured, even voice, 'do come in.' He glanced at Rene's escort. 'That will be all for now, Piet.'

The man mountain retreated back into the corridor and the door closed behind him.

'Monsieur Le Balance,' Rene said respectfully. 'Thank you for seeing me.'

Le Balance played his part in getting the niceties out of the way. 'I am a businessman. And you offered me some very profitable business.' He paused before adding meaningfully, 'Potentially.'

'I think you'll find it profitable enough,' Rene said confidently.

Le Balance moved the conversation straight to business. 'May I see the merchandise?' he asked.

'Of course.' Rene was eager to get business settled so he could be on his way... but only if he was well compensated. 'If I may see the money.'

Le Balance was happy to comply. 'Of course. A very wise attitude.' He picked up a briefcase and placed it on a small table. He opened the top to show that it was filled by taped stacks of bank notes. 'Here it is. Ten million Belgian Francs.'

Rene's eyes widened at the vast fortune in front of him. It was a thousand times more than he could ever have dreamed of possessing. 'Ten million?'

'As agreed with the Russians.' Le Balance looked at Rene with suspicion. 'I do hope you're not going to try to increase the price at this late moment.'

'No, no,' Rene replied quickly. He did not want to risk losing such a vast sum of money. 'A deal is a deal.'

That appeased the broker. 'A commendable attitude.'

Rene continued with the friendly discussion. It was best to get this all done as amicably as possible. 'Well, you offered to help me get out of Belgium. That kind of kindness demands some loyalty.'

That actually seemed to please the broker. 'It's a shame you're leaving Brussels,' he said sadly. 'You're the sort of man I could use.' He paused for a moment before getting back to business. 'Now, shall we get on? The notebook?'

'Of course.' Rene fished the little book from his pocket and showed it to Le Balance – though at a distance which was both distant enough to be safe enough for him and close enough not to insult his host. 'Here it is.'

'May I have a look?' Le Balance asked, extending a hand.

Rene considered for a second. Le Balance was a decent host – but he was also known to have been responsible for the deaths of more than a dozen men. Offending him by refusing would not be wise. Then again, the broker could have just had Piet come back and take the book, but he had asked. Rene handed the notebook across. 'Here.'

'Thank you.' Le Balance took the book and swiftly flicked through it. 'Yes. Yes,' he nodded to himself, 'this is exactly what I expected. And what my buyer in London hoped for.' He tapped a telegram on the table on front of him absently and a smile spread across his face. 'I may even turn a profit on this transaction.'

That made Rene laugh. 'You wouldn't have agreed to meet me if you didn't expect a healthy return.' Rene was sure that the mysterious buyer's name was on the telegram.

Rene's words caused no offence. In fact, Le Balance was quite complimented by them. 'You know my reputation.'

'I do,' Rene nodded, before moving to an equally pressing matter. 'When I contacted you, you said that you could get me out of the country.'

'Of course,' Le Balance nodded. He lifted an envelope from the table and showed Rene the contents. 'I have train tickets to the Dutch coast and then on a ferry to England. You can be hidden amongst the English by morning. Oh, and there's a passport from the Netherlands as well under the name Johann van Mesner. Your travel documents are for that name.' He passed the envelope to Rene, who accepted it gratefully.

'Thank you.'

Le Balance's attention had now shifted almost entirely to the notebook as he flicked through it, reading a few lines before moving to another page. 'Oh, I should thank you.'

'Actually, I should thank you both.'

Le Balance and Rene both stopped short at the unexpected sound of a cultured female voice. They turned to see who had spoken and saw an attractive blonde woman standing by the window. The floor length curtains rippled in the breeze from the suddenly open window.

'Who the devil are you?' Le Balance demanded.

'I'm the competition,' replied the blonde woman. Though neither man knew it, this was the assassin who was travelling most recently under the name Ilsa Lund.

'For him or for me?' Rene asked.

She replied with a cold humourless smile. 'For both of you. I'll take the book – and the money.'

Le Balance was on edge but showed no sign of actual fear. 'And if we say no?'

"Ilsa Lund" tilted her head quizzically. 'Do I really have to answer that?'

Le Balance spread his hands to show he was no threat. 'I assume it involves mindless violence and senseless brutality?'

'And a good deal of blood,' Ilsa Lund nodded. 'None of it mine.'

Le Balance looked to the petty crook by his side. 'What do you think Monsieur LeVal?'

Rene recognised that this woman had a confidence and arrogance which made him nervous and his experiences during the war had taught him not to underestimate women... and yet his nature made him want to dismiss her as *just a woman*. Deep down he didn't believe for a second that a woman could beat a criminal's professional muscle. 'I think you should get Piet and his friends to help her leave through a window.'

Le Balance nodded thoughtfully. 'I think you might be right.'

Ilsa Lund shook her head and then nodded at the door. As she did they all became aware of the violent sounds of fighting coming from the corridor.

'That noise is your shaved gorillas outside,' Ilsa said. 'I imagine the back-up Russian team have found them. Hopefully they'll all kill each other. If not, I'll deal with whatever's left.'

Rene started to feel more uneasy with the arrival of another faction. He hadn't anticipated that and it could ruin his plans.

The window to the side of the room exploded inwards, spraying glass shredding the heavy drapes. Instinctively the three occupants of the room threw themselves to the ground.

'What the hell?' Rene was the first to climb to his feet, looking at the familiar male figure climbing in through what was left of the window.

'Who's this?' Le Balance asked.

It was the man in the window who replied. 'The one *he* stole that book from,' he said, indicating Rene. He extended his hand to the broker. 'If you don't mind.'

'Oh, but I do object,' Le Balance said.

'So do I,' Ilsa said resolutely.

The suited man looked at the three other occupants of the room. 'Well, this could be unfortunate.'

Andy and Helena entered *L'Hotel du Presidente* and entered with a swagger and confidence neither felt. They were both acutely aware that the majority of the clientele in the hotel were considerably more staid in their fashion than they were. However, they ignored the questioning eyes and carried on their way.

'Style it out,' Helena hissed.

Andy nodded, full of faux confidence. 'We can blag our way through.' She pressed the button to summon the lift.

'We'd better get our arses in gear and do it quickly,' Helena said. Her eyes were on a prissy looking man in an overly neat hotel uniform hurrying towards them. 'I don't think he's keen on us being here.'

'He's not alone there,' Andy grumbled. The lift doors opened and she ushered Helena inside. She quickly pressed the button for the floor Erimem's grandfather had mentioned and as the doors slid shut she forced a cheesy grin at the irate hotel worker and waved a cheeky goodbye.

'That was unnecessary,' Helena said coolly.

Andy nodded. She kept her gaze straight ahead, not looking at her friend. 'You did exactly the same, didn't you?'

'Yep.'

'Well done,' Andy said. 'Proud of you.'

The lift rose smoothly until the doors slid open – and ahead of them was a pitched battle being fought by six huge, muscular men. A couple of the men held knives but most of the fighting was hand to hand and utterly brutal. Punches were aimed at throats, others were thrown were the middle knuckle raised to cause permanent damage to an eye if they hit. Kicks slammed into stomachs and faces, and every blow was met with something equally vicious in reply.

'Sod me sideways,' Andy muttered. 'This is not the Swinging Sixties.'

'Oh this is nothing,' Helena argued. 'You should have seen what it was like when fans of the Beatles and the Stones got into an argument over who was better.'

'Did you just say the Who were better?'

Helena scowled. 'Not the first time I've heard that joke.'

'Sorry,' Andy said insincerely.

'So where do we have to go?' Helena asked.

Andy pointed towards the far end of the corridor beyond the struggling mass of humanity. 'End door.'

'It bloody would be,' Helena grumbled. Her eyebrows rose. 'Ready to kick some arse?'

'I'd rather go to the bar, but if I absolutely have to…'

It turned out that Andy *did* have to. Helena threw herself into the fray, punching and pushing her way through the melee. 'Excuse me. Pardon me. Lady coming through.' She punctuated her words with a solid punch to a Russian groin.

The Russian shrieked but Helena was already moving on.

Andy stopped long enough to say, 'She's not much of a lady, sorry.' For added effect she kicked the Russian in the groin as well, then she hurried after Helena.

The fight was untidy and unstructured with bodies rebounding off walls and fists flying hard. However, Helena and Andy did eventually make it to the door at the end of the corridor.

'One out of five review on Trip Adviser,' Helena said.

Andy agreed. 'If you're travelling to 1967 Brussels, don't pick this place.'

Helena was already trying to open the door but it remained resolutely shut. 'Locked.'

Andy shrugged. 'Only one thing for it.'

They both stepped back and kicked hard at the door.

The door burst inwards. Rene and Le Balance turned sharply, startled to see two young women standing in the doorway.

'Who the devil are you?' Le Balance spluttered.

'Charlie's Angels!' Andy answered.

'Wrong decade,' Helena hissed. 'We're more Cathy Gale and Emma Peel.'

Andy knew her classic TV and approved of Helena's choice. 'We're them too.'

The blonde woman in the room looked at the two newcomers with surprise and disdain. 'What are you two wittering about?' She seemed rather annoyed that this intrusion had halted whatever was happening in the room very suddenly.

For Andy and Helena that delay was more than useful. It allowed them to take stock of the room, the four people in it, how the sides within the room were pitted against each other and who was allied with who. It took just a fraction of a second to recognise that everybody there was looking out solely for themselves.

Andy offered her cheesiest grin to the blonde woman. 'Don't ask us what we're doing. We're winging it.'

A frown creased the blonde woman's elegant brow. 'Are you idiots?'

Helena shrugged and her mouth quirked into a sort of facial shrug too. 'That's a very fair question, really.'

'I suppose it is,' Andy agreed with a slow nod before giving a brief sigh. 'No, we're just here to make sure things don't go skew-wiff.'

'And make sure the British agent gets the notebook back,' Helena added before looking at the neat thirty-something in the Saville Row suit. 'That would be you, suit boy?'

The suited man replied in a smooth, educated and slightly superior British voice. 'How did you know?'

'Wild guess,' Andy answered. She cast her eyes around the others in the room.' Guessing you're the broker, you're the dodgy sleaze who pinched the book,' her eyes found the blonde woman, 'and you are...'

Helena nudged her. 'Control yourself.'

'Please,' Andy snorted, 'I'm a married woman.' She scrutinised the blonde, taking in the nasty-looking pistol she held in her hand. 'And I'd say you are trouble.'

The blonde shrugged. 'You're right,' she answered. And she swung her gun upwards.

The room was suddenly filled with the sound gunfire, as all four participants in the action had pistols in their hands and were firing at each other. Helena grabbed Andy and dragged her behind a two hundred year old *chaise longue*. From their position they could see that they had been right - there were no allies in the room. Every one of the combatants was on their own, each of them trying to find some kind of cover. Bullets flew in every direction, making Andy and Helena duck back behind the antique *chaise*.

'Jesus H Corbett!' Andy exclaimed. 'How many fights are going on in here?' She started to poke her head up from behind the *chaise* but Helens dragged her back.

'Get down!'

More bullets whistled through the air.

Erimem and Fiona Docherty met Adam and David outside of the *Drouthy Duck*, a smart looking pub in a little lane just off of Princes Street. Fiona had explained the meaning of "Drouthy" and that the place was named after legendary pub in the Highlands.

'Ready to eat?' David asked.

Fiona looked at her husband with a scowl that managed to be both disapproving and affectionate. 'You only just ate breakfast.'

David refused to be cowed. 'I'm a growing laddie.'

Fiona patted her husband's stomach. 'Growing in the wrong directions.'

David grumbled about the disgrace of body shaming but did so with a smile.

Erimem liked the way the older couple acted together. They were comfortable and relaxed and obviously adored each other. That was not the kind of relationship she had seen from her own parents. Her father had been the great and mighty Pharaoh Amenhotep, the ruler of the world and a living god while her mother had been one of his army of wives. She had only ever seen her mother and father together two or three times and there had been none of this love she saw in Adam's parents. She had never thought anything was strange about her childhood. It was the only one she had ever experienced but seeing this kind of family life she did wonder at how different her life would have been if she had been born into this modern world or even into a peasant life with two parents around her every day instead of nurses, handmaidens and once she had reached her teen years, Antranak and his soldiers as she had bullied and cajoled them into teaching her to be a warrior.

'Why question your past?'

Erimem heard the voice and looked blankly at her three companions. None of them had spoken. Adam was just wearing a happy grin watching his parents bicker playfully. That brought a rush of something to Erimem. A warmth she had rarely felt before, but she had to push that aside for a moment. She knew what was about to happen.

Erimem caught Adam's arm and leaned close. 'Is there somewhere I can be alone for a minute?' she whispered.

Adam looked at her blankly for a moment. He didn't understand what she meant but she raised her eyebrows.

'Grandfather,' she said.

That answered any questions he had. 'Okay.' He took Erimem's hand and glanced at his parents. 'Nip inside and get a table. We'll be with you in five.'

David Docherty looked disappointed. 'I'm hungry.'

Adam pointed Erimem towards a doorway. 'In there.' as he she off he turned back to his parents and lowered his voice. 'I think she saw something she wants to get for you.'

'Oh, she doesn't need to do that,' Fiona protested, though Adam could see his mother adding another plus in her opinion of Erimem.

He shrugged. 'She's like that and I'm not brave enough to argue with her.'

'We'll get that table,' David said and opened the door for Fiona to enter. 'But remember, five minutes.'

'Five minutes,' Adam agreed, before hurrying to catch up with Erimem. She was in the doorway of a quiet little shop. 'You still here?'

'He is coming,' she answered.

Adam took her hand. 'We need to buy my parents a present or I've lied to them.'

And then the doorway was gone. In its place was a Mediterranean harbour with fishing boats. The clothes worn by the fishermen clearly said that they had travelled back into the distant past.

Erimem looked at Adam with surprise. 'What are you doing here?'

'Nice to see you, too,' Adam answered.

Erimem shook her head, clearly annoyed with herself for sounding so short with him. 'I'm sorry. It's just that I have never had anyone join me in these visions before.'

'I brought him here,' an old man said from behind them.

'Why?' Erimem asked bluntly. She looked at the old pharaoh with a mixture of affection and suspicion.

The old man squeezed her hand. 'It's lovely to see you too.' He turned to Adam. 'She's my favourite grand-daughter.'

'I am your *only* grand-daughter,' Erimem pointed out.

Her grandfather waved way her concern. 'Don't be picky, child.' He turned to Adam and scrutinised him as if he was a farmer eyeing up livestock. 'So, you're the young rogue with designs on my grand-daughter, eh?' He leaned closer. 'Are your intentions honourable?'

Adam looked like a deer in the headlights. 'Er, yes, sir, your pharaoh... sir.'

The old man sniffed. 'Then you're not as clever as I thought you were. How very disappointing.'

Adam replied without thinking. 'Listen, I'm stuck in somebody else's head talking to her grandad who might or might not ever have existed and who definitely croaked more than three thousand years before I was born, so gimme a break, okay?'

The old pharaoh stared at the younger man. 'Not many people would talk to a pharaoh like that.' There was more than a hint of a threat in that old voice. 'Fewer still would be so quarrelsome with a man who can do *this*.' He waved his hand in the air... and suddenly it was night at the harbour, with lamp and lanterns offering the only light other than the reflections on the water.

Adam refused to back down. 'Pretty sure I saw David Blaine do that trick on telly last month.'

The old man glared at him for a long moment and then a broad, if somewhat lacking in teeth, grin spread across his face. As his smile widened, the sky brightened until it was the height of a sunny day again. 'I like him,' the old pharaoh said to Erimem. 'You can keep him.'

Erimem looked at his grandfather disapprovingly. 'He is not a pet,' she said.

'I know,' the old man sniffed. 'Pets aren't allowed to sleep on your bed.'

Erimem's eyes widened in surprise. 'I'm not sure I should be talking about that with my grandfather.'

Her grandfather laughed. 'I have no objections. I was young myself once.' He shrugged. 'Actually, I was young more than once.'

Erimem tried to pull the conversation to more comfortable ground. 'I am sure my love life is not why you have brought us here.'

'*Love* life, eh?' the old pharoah murmured. 'Things must be getting serious.'

'Grandfather,' Erimem glowered at him, 'you are a very annoying man.'

'That's what your friend Andy said,' the pharaoh answered.

Mention of her friend immediately changed Erimem's attitude. 'When did you see Andy?' she demanded. 'And why?'

The old man scuffed his sandalled feet and nonchalantly kicked a pebble into the water. 'Well, you were busy and I had a little task that needed doing...'

'So you sent my friend?' Erimem sounded angry.

It was water off a duck's back to her grandfather. 'Friends,' he corrected her. 'Helena went with her.' His wispy eyebrows rose. 'She is the old one, isn't she?'

Adam winced. 'Well, that's rude.'

The pharaoh shrugged. 'Nothing wrong with being old. I'm not exactly young myself.'

'And I swear that you will get no older if my friends are harmed,' Erimem snapped. She pushed her anger aside and forced herself to focus. 'Where have you sent them and why have you summoned us?'

'Brussels, 1967,' her grandfather replied. 'I needed them to save the world.' He shrugged. 'But I think they could do with some help.'

'Your timing is terrible!' Erimem exploded. 'We're about to have lunch with Adam's parents!'

'Oh, the in-laws,' the old fellow chuckled. 'I must meet them some time soon.' Erimem just glared at him. 'Well, we'll sort that out later. The good thing with time travel is that you can do this and still be back in time for your lunch.'

'Or we could get killed fifty-odd years ago,' Adam pointed out.

'Oh, don't do that,' the old Pharaoh advised. 'If you do it might mean the end of the world and then nobody would get any lunch.'

'Christ on a bike,' Adam muttered to Erimem, 'you weren't joking about him being annoying, were you?'

'No,' Erimem sighed, 'I really wasn't.' She turned to her grandfather. 'Tell us what we need to know.'

Erimem blinked.

Beside her, Adam also blinked as his consciousness returned to his body. He winced at the sudden pain in his skull.

'Shit a brick!' he hissed, 'do you feel this every time he talks to you?'

Erimem shook her head. 'Not really, but I don't have to visit someone else's brain.'

Adam blinked a few times. His head started to clear. 'Back to your place?' he asked.

Erimem nodded and gripped the middle band of the ring on her thumb. Adam reached for the matching ring he wore as well.

A spitting ball of electricity filled the little doorway for an instant. As it faded away, the doorway was empty.

Less than thirty metres away, Fiona and David Docherty had found a free table and were taking their seat in the *Drouthy Duck* pub. They had no idea that Erimem and their son were further away than they could ever have believed was possible.

CHAPTER FOUR

There was chaos in Le Balance's hotel room. The five way fight in the suite had been joined by the battle from the corridor outside. The scene was more reminiscent of a western saloon than a prestigious European hotel.

'Can you see…?' Helena's sentence was cut short as a decanter filled with very fine sherry sailed over her head and smashed against the wall not far behind her. 'Forget I asked.'

A gun went off and Andy risked peering out of cover. She winced at the chaos. 'We have got to start arming ourselves for shenanigans like this.'

'Shenanigans?' Helena asked, wide-eyed. 'You call this shenanigans?'

'What do you want me to call it?' Andy blurted. 'Malarkey?'

Two more shots sounded in quick succession.

'How about insanity?' Helena offered.

Andy shrugged. 'Sounds about right.' She peered around the room again. 'You any idea where that book is?'

Helena's gaze focused on Rene LeVal. 'Pretty sure he's got it.'

'Okay,' Andy nodded. 'Let's grab him and get the F out of here.'

Helena liked the sound of that plan. 'Right,' she said. 'We grab him, zap him back to the Habitat and then get the notebook from him.'

'Do we get to beat him up a bit for causing us all this hassle?' Andy asked hopefully.

'No need,' Helena answered. 'He'll be having the screaming hab-dabs at being beamed away through time and space.'

'Fair point,' Andy conceded. 'Are we ready to…'

She didn't finish her sentence.

The *chaise longue* they were hiding behind suddenly lurched towards them, toppling over as another pair of men entered the room.

Andy scrambled to her feet. 'Who the hell are they?' she muttered.

'No idea,' Helena said, pulling herself to her feet. 'No idea where our boy's gone either.'

The arrival of these newcomers had thrown the room into even deeper confusion. Andy tried to look around for LeVal but her attention was caught by the approach of a sweaty man-mountain who was already bleeding from the nose and mouth. She jumped aside just in time for him to miss her completely and slam violently into the wall, hard enough for Andy to wince.

'Oh, that's going to nip.'

The man had been pushed by the guard Rene had earlier discovered was Piet – and with fighting going on all around him, Piet's suspicious eyes were now on these two young women.

Helena held up his hand to calm him down. 'You can't hit us. We are poor meek women and this is 1967 when real men would not do such a thing.'

Piet just frowned.

Helena shrugged. 'Yeah, look, I know it's bollocks but then again, so is my friend's target.'

Andy took the cue and kicked Piet hard in the groin.

A strangulated whimper came from Piet's mouth and his knees dipped but he didn't fall. His hand shot out and he caught Andy's hair in a great paw.

Helena swung possibly the best punch of her long life and felt Piet's nose break but he didn't waver. He rag-dolled Andy and threw her backwards, raising his fist to swing it at Helena.

And then suddenly he was following the other gorilla in lurching forward and slamming into the wall. Erimem and Adam stood behind the position Piet had been standing in.

Helena felt a smile of relief spread across her face. 'Fancy seeing you here.'

Erimem didn't answer. She swept up a metal drinks tray from a table and stepped forward fast, slamming it hard across Piet's face as the thug tried to turn back towards them. She beat him about the head with it four or five more times before he fell to the ground. She looked at the buckled tray which clearly showed the dents made by Piet's skull then shrugged and dropped it to the floor.

'We can share greetings later,' she said. 'My grandfather sent us to help you.'

'Good old grandad,' Andy said, gratefully accepting Adam's help to get back to her feet. 'He's a pain in the arse, by the way.'

'Yes, he really is,' Erimem agreed, 'but tell us what we need to do.'

'Trying to get a notebook back from a crook,' Helena said, 'but we've sort of lost track of him in the fight.' Her eyes widened and she looked towards Adam. 'Behind you.'

The policeman turned just in time to punch the Russian agent charging at him squarely in the jaw. The Russian stumbled back a step and Andy kicked the back of his knee making him topple backwards. Andy swung another vicious kick at him as he hit the floor.

'Thanks,' Adam said automatically.

Through a shattered window the unmistakable sound of sirens began to wail. The first to react to the noise was Le Balance. He had many of the city's police on his payroll, but he wouldn't be able to play this down easily. He looked around, searching for Rene and the briefcase.

He turned just in time to see the briefcase an instant before it slammed into his face, knocking him unconscious.

Rene tightened his grip on the briefcase and quickly pulled the black book from Le Balance's grip. He grabbed the broker's telegram, too.

There was no way out through the door but as he looked round, Rene saw the cable dangling just outside the shattered window. That was how the Englishman had come in.

Moving quickly to the window, Rene grabbed one of the thick sashes tying the drapes back and wrapped it several times round his hand. Gripping the cable he pushed out from the windowsill. He gripped the cable with all the strength he could muster while still clinging to the briefcase. Memories of abseiling down walls to plant bombs on German military installations came back to him and his body responded, helping him lower his way down the outside of the hotel in a quick but controlled way. He ignored the startled pedestrians who looked at him with shock as he reached the ground and threw away the now tattered curtain sash. Despite the thick material doing its job his palm was red and he felt the burning ache in it. He ignored the pain and hurried to the nearest taxi and got in. A few seconds later the car pulled away.

The police siren had concentrated the action in Le Balance's room. Those who were still able to stand were now looking at their escape strategy. The rest were looking at either the ceiling or the insides of their eyelids.

Looking around the room, Andy saw the handsome dark haired man in his thirties (dangerous if you liked that sort of thing) look at an athletically slim blonde woman of around thirty (also dangerous if you liked that sort of thing – and as it happened Andy did, even if it was only to look at now that she was a respectable married woman with a gorgeous wife at home). The blonde looked back at the suited man and both bolted. The woman sprinted for the door and the man... the man just threw himself out through a shattered window. Andy shrugged. Somehow watching a man hurl himself out of a window had become bog standard for her days. She was relived to catch sight of him clinging to some kind of rope before he disappeared downwards.

Taking another look at the clearing room, Andy spotted the prim, neat fellow who looked appalled at the chaos going on in his elegant rooms. 'That's who we need to talk to,' she told her group.

Erimem and Adam moved in unison, both grabbing Le Balance by the collar and hauling him to his feet. He seemed terrified. That suited Andy and her friends. Fear loosened tongues.

'Where did he go?' Andy demanded of the little man.

The reply was weak. 'Who?'

Andy caught a slight movement from Erimem's eyes towards the window and she understood what her friend meant without a word being exchanged. 'Erimem,' she said casually, 'when was the last time you threw someone out of a window?'

Erimem's nose wrinkled in thought. 'Almost a week,' she answered. 'I think I could use some practice.'

Andy gave Le Balance the most obviously forced smile she could muster. 'Listen, that window is open and if you don't answer our questions quickly and honestly you're leaving through it? Understand?'

'And I will enjoy doing it,' Erimem added for extra menace.

Adam nudged Erimem. 'You could do the whole "This is Sparta" bit and kick him out of the window.'

Erimem frowned. 'This isn't Sparta. It's Brussels.'

'I know,' Adam answered. 'It's a film reference. *300*. Glaswegian Leonidas...'

Erimem couldn't hide her smirk any longer. 'I know,' she said. 'I am just... what's your saying... winding you up.'

Helena tapped Andy's arm. 'Doctor Frankenstein, you have created a monster.'

Andy could see things were beginning to drift. 'Back on topic...' she turned a cold stare to Le Balance. 'Tell us where Rene LeVal went or you take those flying lessons.'

Le Balance looked at his captors and then at the fallen, broken men scattered around his floor. Piet, in particular, looked as if he had stepped in front of a train. The police sirens were now just outside the hotel and he was almost out of time before an escape could be made. Pragmatism won out. 'He will be going to the train station,' the broker said. 'He is booked on a train headed for Rotterdam.'

'Appropriate for a rotten piece of work like him,' Helena said, sounding pleased with herself for the joke.

'Why is he going to Rotterdam?' Erimem asked.

'Good question,' Andy said. Her lips pursed in thought. 'It's a port.'

'So he's booked on a ferry?' Adam mused.

Andy looked sternly at Le Balance. 'You're not off the hook for bouncing out of that window yet.'

Le Balance noted that the police sirens were now alarmingly quiet. That meant the police were in the hotel. 'Today's ferry to Dover,' he said without any hesitation. His eyes widened as he saw that the telegram he had placed on the table was also gone. 'And then he'll go to *Les Ambassadeurs* club to make my sale.' His face slumped. 'And he'll have my money. Twice.'

'There,' Andy beamed, oblivious to the man's loss, 'that wasn't so hard, was it?'

'We should go before the police get here,' Erimem said.

'What am I?' Adam protested. 'Scots mist?'

'All right,' Erimem conceded, 'before the *local* police get here. Is that better?'

Adam nodded. 'Cool. Thank you.'

Andy stared hard at Le Balance. 'Don't send anybody after us.'

'Who can I send? The little man wheedled.' My men are unconscious.'

'That is a fair point,' Erimem said.

Adam's lips pursed thoughtfully. 'Probably better safe than sorry, though.'

In unison, he and Erimem swung punches at Le Balance. They hit him simultaneously, and he slumped to the floor. Somehow he even managed to do that with a hint of elegance and panache.

'Oh, isn't that sweet?' Andy beamed. 'They even punch people together.'

Helena nodded. 'Makes me miss that kind of romance in my marriage. The good old days when we beat up villains together.'

Adam was watching them with his eyebrows raised. 'Are you two finished?'

'For now, probably,' Helena said, 'but we'll hit you with more teasing later.'

'And we'll probably take the piss out of you as well,' Andy grinned.

Erimem indicated the window. The police sirens were, one by one, becoming silent, clearly indicating tat the cars had pulled up at the hotel. 'Perhaps we should go before the police arrive on this floor?'

'Good idea,' Andy said. 'Let's run like hell.'

Escaping from the hotel proved remarkably simple. They took the stairs and simply went up one flight before coming down as the police reached the floor on which Le Balance's rooms were situated. The police simply waved them on and impatiently told them to hurry and get out of the way. A few minutes later they were standing on the street in front of the hotel.

'What is the best way to the train station?' Erimem asked. 'Do we know?'

Helena nodded. 'I think I do.'

'But how do we get there?' Adam asked.

Erimem's eyes fell on an empty police car. She looked at Andy and Helena, who shrugged.

'Shame not to use it if it's there,' Helena said.

Andy nodded. 'And we can't be pinching from the police because we have a copper with us.'

Adam's eyebrows lifted. 'And how well do you think that will stand up in court?'

Andy shrugged. 'Don't ask me. I make sandwiches for a living.'

Helena shook her head. 'And I'm a very old lady.'

All Erimem could offer was a wry smile. 'And I am even older than her.'

The piled into the police car with a grumbling Adam slumping into the back seat beside Erimem. 'You're nutters,' he muttered, 'all three of you. Complete nutters!'

'Guilty as charged,' Andy agreed happily as Helena started the engine and quickly pulled out into traffic.

'Lights and sirens?' Andy asked hopefully.

Helena gave a very false and forced glower. 'How old are you?'

Adam's voice came from the back seat. 'You're never too old for sirens.'

Helena sighed and operated the controls to start the sirens and light on top of the car. 'Kids,' she muttered good-naturedly.

Erimem shook her head but couldn't hide her grin. She nudged Adam's arm. 'And you called us nutters.'

Even though she was working from memory and out of practice driving on the right, Helena moved the car through the streets quickly, even coming to enjoy the sight of people making sure to give them a wide berth when they heard the wail of the sirens.

They abandoned the police car in a small side street across from Brussels' main train station, *Gare de Bruxelles-Central*, or as it was more widely known, Brussels Central.

They ran into the station and waited impatiently while Andy queued to buy tickets for the train on which Rene LeVal was booked to travel. She quickly returned with tickets.

'I thought that would take longer,' Erimem said. She sounded impressed.

Andy wrinkled her nose. 'It did take ages,' she confessed. 'I queued for twenty minutes then found we needed passports, so I popped back to the Habitat for those and a load of money.' She nodded back at the queue where she could see the back of he own head. 'See? I'm still queueing. In about thirty seconds, Erimem is going to tell me – I mean that me in the queue - that you're all going to wait for me out of sight. Just so there's not two of me about.'

The alarming thing was that this seemed to be quite a normal thing for them to talk about, but Erimem did as suggested and talked to the other version of her friend, before the party moved off in the direction of the platform their train would be departing from.

The conductor at their carriage met them with suspicion and a noticeable amount of condescension. 'This carriage is reserved for First Class passengers only.'

All four waved their tickets in the man's face.

'Just as well we're stinking rich, isn't it?' Andy said cheekily.

Adam just shrugged and nodded at Erimem. 'You expect a member of a royal family to travel anything less than First Class?'

The conductor began to apologise but the little party was already bounding up onto the train.

Helena led the way along the very well-appointed carriage until she reached their prescribed seats. She gave a very contented moan. 'I may steal these seats for the house.'

'Comfy A-F,' Andy agreed as Erimem and Adam took their seats opposite. 'I suppose this is where we work out a cunning plan.'

'Guess so, Baldrick,' Adam agreed.

Erimem shook her head. 'There is no need. Andy has already made our plan for us.'

'I have?' Andy was confused by that. 'I mean, I know it's probably brilliant and incisive, but would you mind reminding me what it is again?' She grinned cheesily at her friend.

Erimem pointed at the door at the back of the carriage. 'You booked us at the front of the train. We can work our way methodically to the back until we find your villain, LeVal.'

Andy threw her hands up in protest. 'He's not mine,' she protested. 'He's your spooky grandad's.'

'All right,' Erimem conceded, 'my annoying spooky grandfather's villain.'

Andy's cheeks puffed out and she sniffed. 'We can't do anything till we leave the station and get moving at a fair lick of pace or he'll just jump off.'

'So?' Erimem asked.

Andy raised a hand and waved to one of the stewards. 'So we might as well make the most of not being the hoi polloi.' She smiled at the conductor – thankfully not the one who had annoyed her as they had boarded. 'Could we possibly have four glasses of champagne, please?'

'But of course,' the conductor smiled before disappearing from view.

Helena's lips pursed in thought. 'I'd say it might be early in the day but I've no idea what time our body clocks are running on.'

'It's a big world,' Andy sniffed. 'It's got to be champagne o'clock somewhere.' She smiled as the conductor sent a steward towards their seats, a silver tray in his hand with four flutes of champagne resting on top of it.

A few compartments away, Rene LeVal had settled into a seat in the corner. His eyes focused on the door. What he didn't know was that he had not escaped to the train station as completely as he had hoped. In addition to Erimem's party in First Class, there were several other parties on the train intent on taking the notebook from him.

CHAPTER FIVE

The train had pulled out of Brussels Central precisely on time, which had led to the inevitable snarky comments from Erimem's friends.

'A train running on time?' Andy frowned. 'How terribly un-British. Does not compute.'

'We are not in Britain, remember,' Erimem said.

'European trains are usually pretty reliable,' Adam offered. 'I bummed around Europe on trains for a few summers when I was a laddie.'

Helena agreed. 'Plus, this is the Sixties and things hadn't gone to pot.' She wrinkled her nose and shrugged. 'Actually, a lot of my friends *had* turned to pot in the Sixties.' Her eyes drifted off into her memories. 'You could get high just saying hello to some people.'

Adam's brow furrowed. 'Remembering that I'm Polis, should I be getting the Drug Squad to raid your house?'

Andy nudged Helena. 'Isn't he all Scottish with his "Polis"?'

'He *is* Scottish,' Erimem pointed out, 'and we are supposed to be in Scotland just now. Shopping and having lunch with his Scottish parents.'

Adam tried again. 'Given that I am a police officer,' he said to Helena, 'should I send the boys round to nick you?'

'Nah.' Helena shook her head. 'Smell of the stuff makes me want to heave. I was rubbish at the Sixties. Didn't do any drugs and skipped the free love because I was waiting for Ibrahim.'

'You waited all those years for Ibrahim?' Andy's eyes widened. 'Poor sod wouldn't have known what hit him when you eventually got your hands on him.'

Helena waggled her eyebrows. 'Just as well I'm a doctor, isn't it?'

Andy raised her glass in a salute. 'I hope you had oxygen on standby.'

'Oxygen and a defibrillator in case his heart gave out,' Helena agreed, taking another sip of champagne. 'Happy days.'

Adam coughed. 'This is veering towards TMI. I've got to look Ibrahim in the face after this.'

'Welcome to girl talk,' Andy said. 'You should hear what we say about you.'

He shook his head resolutely. 'I absolutely do *not* want to hear what you all say about me.'

Helena looked out of the window at the swiftly-passing scenery, then sighed and set her champagne down. 'Well, this has all been rather lovely, but...'

Erimem nodded. 'We have a task to do here,' she said firmly, 'we must save history – because I have lunch plans.'

'That kind of dilutes the heroic message, hon,' Andy said honestly.

'It's true, though,' Adam offered. 'My folks are sitting in a really good pub in Edinburgh fifty-odd years from now waiting for us.'

Andy's cheeks puffed out. 'That's a hell of a long wait.'

That pushed Erimem to her feet. 'Then we must begin our work. Find the rat-faced man, get the book from him...'

'...and then go back to lunch with the out-laws,' Andy interrupted. She glanced at Adam. 'No offence.'

'None taken,' he answered.

Andy smiled gratefully. 'And while you party it up in Edinburgh, we'll head home and watch *Homes Under The Hammer*.'

'Because that's how we roll,' Helena nodded. She leaned close to Andy. 'Do people still say "That's how we roll?", by the way?'

Andy shrugged. 'Don't ask me. I am also an old, married woman, you know.'

Erimem led the way through the carriage. 'We should be as quiet an inconspicuous as possible.'

Helena just raised an eyebrow.

'All right,' Erimem conceded. 'We are not good at being inconspicuous.'

'We'll do the best we can,' Adam promised.

'Good.' Erimem turned back to the carriage but then stopped and leaned closer to Adam. 'And then remind me that I must get a present for your mother.'

Rene LeVal sat in his seat and watched the countryside pass by the window. He had not expected to feel any nostalgia at seeing that beautiful scenery, dragging him back to his days during the war when this was where he hid, where he fought and where he caroused with his women. He hadn't anticipated having such a strong emotional reaction to seeing the countryside again after so long in the city. Perhaps it was because he knew that when he left his homeland he would never be able to return. This was the last time he would ever see Belgium.

But Rene could deal with that.

Money and a new house in the Bahamas would soon make the homesickness pass.

As long as he got out of Belgium in one piece and avoided any of Jacques Fournee's men. He was far more worried about his boss and the thugs he employed than any of those fools who had gate-crashed his meeting with Le Balance.

Fournee knew the city and soon enough he would get to Le Balance and find out where Rene was going. But he also knew that if he got to the ferry on time, Fournee's men wouldn't have the opportunity to get to England ahead of him and Britain was a very big place for them to find one man who knew how to hide.

Yes, Rene liked his chances of getting out of this in one piece...

...in one piece and very rich.

The train was fairly quiet and Rene hadn't seen any familiar faces from Fournee's operation boarding the train.

As the locomotive put more and more miles between Rene and Brussels, he began to relax.

He had pulled off his greatest scam and he was going to get away with it.

Unfortunately for Rene, he was not as observant as he thought he was. While he was correct that none of Fournee's men had boarded the train, he had not seen the suited man, from whom he had first stolen the book, slip onto the train and take a seat in another compartment barely ten yards behind Rene. A simple disguise of an overcoat and a trilby had been enough to deceive Rene.

The suited man was not the only problem for Rene that had managed to board the train. The woman who called herself Ilsa Lund was in the next carriage behind Rene's, biding her time.

In fairness to Rene, she had not seen the suited man board the train either. As she sat and worked out her plan for dealing with Rene she hadn't noticed the two dull-looking mean in mundane suits. They looked like salesmen on their way to a meeting. It was a testament to their skill that no-one noticed the slight bulge on their left hips where their pistols rested in holsters. They were experienced men, employed by a Corsican crime family, and they had been diverted from their job of reminding a French politician of his promises to the family, here to Brussels to chase a larger prize. They too were working out their plan for catching Rene.

With Erimem and her friends ahead and three different sets of hostiles behind him, Rene LeVal was about to find out that he hadn't got away with his heist yet.

* * * * *

The tranquillity of Rene LeVal's train journey disintegrated into chaos within the space of just a few seconds.

He had deliberately chosen to sit by the window looking out into the train's corridor. Instinct would have suggested that he should sit in the farthest corner away from the corridor and the door, but Rene knew better than that. Anyone searching for him would look to those corners first and being seated by the window gave him some view of the corridor. He had taken a seat looking backwards simply because there was far more of the train behind than ahead, which made the probability of any trouble coming from that direction far more likely. Besides, Rene had never known any trouble to come from First Class before and that was all that was ahead of him.

This was one occasion when experience could not help Rene. Erimem and her friends had no idea that trouble was off limits to First Class passengers.

Rene heard a door open at the end of the carriage leading to First Class. He held a mirror beside the window to see back along the corridor. It was an old trick he had learned during the war and he had always carried a small mirror since.

He recognised the group who entered immediately. They were an unusual assortment of people. The small North African woman, the vaguely Greek-looking woman, the young woman with a flash of colour in her hair and the tall thin pale young man with unfashionably short hair who radiated the aura of a policeman. He had seen them in Le Balance's hotel room. They had looked useful in a fight, but he hadn't seen them wield any weapons. That gave him an advantage. During the skirmish at the hotel, he had lost his Luger but had scooped up a pistol that had been dropped. He recognised it as a Browning, the type used by the British Army. It was reliable and it had stopping power. He had the advantage over whoever these were.

It didn't make sense to face them in this carriage with five other people around. When the shooting started they would panic and he would lose his advantage if they all tried to get out. He had to remove them from the equation.

Rene waited until the little party from First Class looked into a compartment just ahead and quietly slipped out into the corridor.

He had only managed a few steps before a voice halted his progress.

'There he is.'

They were barely six or seven yards away and there was no chance Rene could escape simply by running. They were all younger and fitter then he was.

He spun round and fired blindly with his Browning.

The shot sent the four pursuers to the floor. They dropped for cover and Rene took the opportunity to run.

He heard the woman – the North African one – shout for her friends to follow him. He glanced back and saw that he had gained another half dozen yards on them.

He turned to run. If he could get to the next carriage he could block the door and make his way off the train one way or another.

He hadn't finished turning when he saw a fist hurtling towards his face. He didn't have time to even flinch before the punch slammed into his jaw. He vaguely recognised the suited man he had taken the notebook from looming over him with a bunched fist as he fell.

Rene was barely conscious as he hit the floor and so he missed the next few minutes. Luckily, that meant he missed his head hitting the floor hard, taking him fully into unconsciousness.

'Did he do something to annoy you?' Andy asked the British agent mildly before looking down at the prone figure of Rene.

'Hang on,' Adam said, 'he was at the hotel.'

Helena sniffed. 'He looks like he's been in a few hotels.'

The suited agent looked back at them. He was mildly bemused by their presence. 'Have we met?'

'Only in passing,' Helena answered.

The agent eyed her like a lion looking at a gazelle. 'Pity,' he said before reluctantly returning his attention to Rene. 'May I ask what your interest in our friend here is?'

'He stole something,' Andy said. 'Our job is to return it to its rightful owner.'

'Then you're in luck,' the agent said. 'I am its rightful owner. At least, I'm the person he stole it from.'

'And your name is?' Adam asked.

The agent raised an eyebrow. 'Is it any of your business?'

'It is if it's John Mason,' Andy answered, 'and we're pretty sure it is.'

The agent nodded. 'That's certainly the name I'm going by,' he agreed. 'Are you from MI6?'

Helena answered. 'Not quite but we were sent to get that book back to you.'

Mason weighed the situation before kneeing and going through Rene's pockets, searching for the notebook. 'I wish all out our agents looked like you.'

'I know you think that's charming,' Andy said, screwing her face up, 'but it's really given me the ick. Honestly, I almost threw up in my mouth.'

Her reaction surprised Mason. 'I definitely wasn't talking to *you.*'

'You keep telling yourself that,' Andy answered.

Mason continued searching for the notebook. 'Do you have a plan for getting off the train?'

Helena's answer was lacking any of glibness. 'Yes, but…' She pointed a finger at the corridor behind Mason.

Mason turned and saw the woman calling herself Ilsa Lund standing behind him, a Baretta aimed at his head. 'But I think you need to hand over the book before you get off, Mr… Mason is it?'

Mason slowly eased himself up to his feet. 'That depends which name you're using today.'

That almost brought a smirk to Ilsa's face. 'You are nobody to talk about that.'

Mason shrugged nonchalantly. 'We both have so many. Who are you today? Alicia Huberman? Doctor Constance Petersen.'

'Ilsa Lund.'

Andy frowned at the mention of the name. 'Why do they ring a bell?'

It was Helena who answered. 'They're all characters played by Ingrid Berman in films.'

'Okay,' Andy nodded, 'she's got taste. I'll give her that.'

'She's also got a gun,' Adam said softly. 'Just thought I'd mention it in case nobody's noticed.'

'We've all noticed,' Helena said. 'We were just trying not to mention it.'

'Thanks for blowing that, LeStrade,' Andy grouched.

'Oh, sorry,' Adam said, 'but not talking about it wasn't likely to make her forget she had it.'

'Who is this woman?' Erimem asked, staring hard at Ilsa. 'She has a killer's eyes.'

'Oh, she *is* a killer,' Mason said. 'She used to be an agent for a foreign power but she's freelance now. He smiled pleasantly at Ilsa. 'Who's paying you for the book?'

She shook her head in reply. 'There's no need for you to know.'

'Well, quite,' Mason said casually, 'because I'm not giving you the book.'

Ilsa's lips curled into an unpleasant snarl of a smile and she raised her Baretta to aim at Mason's head. 'Because you'll be dead.'

'They've definitely done it,' Andy said.

The statement took Ilsa completely by surprise. 'What?'

'You and him,' Andy explained, nodding certainly. 'You have definitely played hide the sausage.'

Ilsa's rage escalated a notch or two. 'Shut up,' she hissed.

'She is correct,' Erimem said thoughtfully. 'Your body language is unmistakable.'

Mason just shrugged helplessly. 'The secret's out.'

'Meeting your ex at work.' Andy shook her head in mock sympathy. 'Well, this is awkward.'

Ilsa met the taunting with anger. 'It won't be awkward when I shoot him in the head and take the book.'

The threat didn't impress Helena. 'If you were going to do that you'd have done it by now.'

'After he gives me the book,' Ilsa said coldly.

Mason held his empty hands out wide. 'I don't seem to have the notebook.'

'Then I assume our Belgian friend still has it.' Ilsa jerked her head towards Rene. 'Take it out of his pocket.'

'Which one is it in?' Mason asked politely.

'I don't know,' Ilsa said. 'Check – but do it slowly and carefully.'

Mason smirked. 'I remember the last time you said that.'

Ilsa glared at him with cold hatred. 'You were never funny or charming.'

'That's not what you said in Bucharest,' Mason said genially.

Ilsa remained unimpressed. 'You're stalling.'

'I was hoping you wouldn't notice,' Mason said ruefully.

'May I ask what is going on out here?' A priest, dressed in the traditional full collar shirt and cassock with a crucifix hanging on his chest, had emerged into the corridor to see what the commotion was. He looked in dismay at the unconscious Rene. 'What have you done to that poor man?'

'Get back inside,' Andy warned the priest.

He ignored her advice and continued to protest. 'Why have you got guns? People are just trying to travel.'

'Get back inside!' Helena roared.

There was a slight commotion behind Ilsa as two men in dull suits nudged their way through.

'Oh, we are so very sorry. We do not mean to interrupt.'

Mason took advantage of the distraction to throw himself at Ilsa. He knocked her gun hand aside and swung a punch at her jaw, but she had already adjusted her position and side-stepped the blow. She pushed forward to meet his own forward motion and drive her forehead into his face. He took a half step backwards but still managed to grab her jacket. Another step backwards pulled her off balance and he twisted, pushing her face into the glass panel looking into the priest's compartment. The glass cracked ominously. Blood began to stain her blonde hair but she ignored it and was on Mason a fraction later. He was considerably bigger and stronger than she was, but she was faster and her smaller size made it easier to move in the confined space of the corridor.

Andy almost moved to join the fight but wasn't sure she would really be all that much assistance. 'Should we help?' she asked.

Erimem shook her head. 'We would only get in the way,' she answered. 'If he wins we do not need to do anything. If she wins we will deal with her.'

Adam tugged at Erimem's arm. 'I don't think they're the immediate problem.'

Helena had also seen what had caught Adam's eye. 'The priest.'

The cleric had dropped to his knees at Rene's side, apparently offering aid, but to anyone paying attention it was clear that he was rifling the unconscious hoodlum's pockets.

'Even for a priest he's a bit handsy,' Andy said.

'Do priests in this world steal from the unconscious?' Erimem asked.

Adam shook his head. 'I don't think he's a real priest.'

The priest looked up sharply, aware that he had been discovered. The benign façade disappeared, replaced by a vicious snarl. He wrenched the crucifix from his chest and twisted the top. A trigger dropped down from the long spar of the cross. As he pointed it at them they could see the black muzzle in its end.

'You have got to be kidding me,' Adam said.

Andy grabbed her friends and pulled them to the floor. 'Get down. That crucifix is loaded.'

The base of the cross flared and the side of the train exploded out in a ball of flames. Through the acrid smoke that filled the corridor they could see the two men in dull suits grappling with the priest.

'They've got him,' Helena said in relief.

Erimem had already noticed that the newcomers had drawn pistols. 'They have also got guns.'

Andy cursed loudly. 'Is there anybody on this train just trying to get to Holland?' she added.

Erimem was already pushing herself towards the fight. 'They must not get the notebook.' She threw herself into the struggle with her friends close behind.

Erimem flew at the two men in suits struggling with the priest and launched herself at them. She had built up a remarkable head of speed in such a short distance and hit one of the suited men with enough impact to drive him backwards. She rolled and sprang to her feet, lashing out one booted foot to catch the suited man's partner in the temple. The priest tried to clamber to his feet but went down again as Adam and Andy barged past him. They were already on the second of the men in suits. Adam gripped the man's wrist, stopping him from raising his pistol while Andy drove the heel of her hand into the man's jaw again and again.

'Bawz tae this,' Adam said eventually. 'I'm Scottish.' He head butted the man, shattering his nose. 'That's how it's done right.'

'Stereotyping much?' Andy asked.

Adam shrugged. 'If you say it, it's racist and stereotyping. If I do it, it's ironic.'

'Incoming!' Andy shouted.

The priest had managed to pluck the book from Rene's pocket but Helena was immediately moving and kicked the book from his hand. The priest squared up to her. From somewhere he had a vicious short blade in his hand. Looking closer, Helena could see it had been hidden under the top of the crucifix.

'Need help?' Adam asked.

'Might do,' Helena answered. 'We'll see.'

Adam's ability to offer assistance disappeared as the dull suit he had attacked kicked his legs out from under him.

The corridor had deteriorated into anarchy with the combatants breaking down into individual fights. Mason and Ilsa struggled for dominance while Helena had just about gained the upper hand on the priest, dodging his blade's razor edge and using a mixture of striking styles to bloody his face. Adam and Andy had managed to subdue their opponent by getting his head in the doorway and slamming the door shut on it, and they looked up to see Erimem duck a punch from her adversary and slide behind him. She caught his hair and drove his face forward into the solid wooden panel between compartments. His knees dipped slightly and she reacted, smashing his head against the wooden surface again and then again. He sagged to the side and she drove his head forward again, only this time it hit the glass of the window looking into a compartment. The glass shattered and he slumped forward. Passengers inside the compartment screamed, but they were ignored. The battle wasn't over yet.

'Where is he?' Erimem demanded. 'LeVal, the one with the book!'

Adam and Andy looked to where Rene Level had been lying. He was gone, and so was the book.

'He's legged it!' Andy shouted.

Helena was distracted for an instant and almost paid for it with her life. The priest's knife arced by in front of her, missing her throat by a fraction, but she reacted swiftly. She had two thousand years of experience to call on and she reacted out of instinct. She caught his wrist, ducked under his arm, twisting as she went, and then pushed forward with all her strength.

The priest looked startled and then fell back, the blade embedded in his chest. It protruded upright like an inverted crucifix. It was somehow apt.

'Just as well I'm not Catholic or I'd be on my knees for a month saying penance for that,' she said, sucking in a breath.

Erimem was already trying to follow Rene. 'We must go after that book.'

Andy caught her arm. 'Look outside.'

They looked out through the damaged side of the carriage. The train was slowing.

'That shouldn't be happening,' Adam said. 'This ground's as flat as a bowling green.'

'Hang on.' Andy halted proceedings briefly and nudged Adam aside. One of the suited men had stumbled to his feet. She caught him by the collar and the back of the trousers before hurling him through the open side of the train. He landed on the steep embankment at the side and bounced down to land in a huge puddle. 'You go for a look outside, mate.'

Adam was clinging to the inside of the train while leaning out as far as he could. He was the first to see the train's engine pulling away into the distance, picking up speed as it went. 'He's cut us loose.'

'What?' Andy humphed. 'The sneaky git.'

Helena nodded sullenly as the train slowed further. 'The engine is still moving but we're dead in the water.'

'What?' The revelation gave a surge of energy to Mason, who finally gained the upper hand over Ilsa and he threw her hard against the wall of the corridor. She groaned and slumped. Mason looked out at the engine disappearing into the distance.' I have to get after...' His voice stopped, his mouth and eyes open wide in shock.

'I'm afraid not, Mr Mason.' Ilsa had pulled herself to her feet and was close behind Mason.

'What have you done?' Helena demanded.

Ilsa pulled her hand back. She was holding a shard of broken glass, a torn piece of cloth around its broader end to act as a handle. The other end was crimson, dripping with Mason's blood. The agent was clutching at his back, but the blood was flowing fast from a deep wound.

Erimem didn't bother with any further questions. Instinct made her attack Ilsa. The heel of her hand slammed into Ilsa's face, high on her cheekbone. The blonde woman reeled back.

'You'll pay for that.'

'Not today.' Andy was scooping up a fallen pistol. 'She's not carrying cash.'

Ilsa quickly took in the scene and then flicked her wrist. Something almost flat flew from her wristwatch and an instant later it exploded in a flare of light and smoke. It only took seconds to clear but that was enough time for Ilsa to have disappeared from the corridor.

Andy looked along the corridor then outside. There was no sign of Ilsa. 'She's gone.'

'At least we know where the rabbit's going,' Adam said, trying to get one last look at the train's engine as it pulled further away.

Helena had turned her attention to Mason. The spy was now also bleeding from the mouth and his knees were buckling. 'Sod the train. This man has been skewered. He's bleeding out.'

That focused everyone's attention on Mason.

'How bad is he?' Erimem asked.

Helena's cursory examination had told her enough. 'Dead if we don't get him to hospital.'

'We're stuck in the middle of nowhere,' Andy reminded her.

Helena pointed at the time travel ring on her finger. 'Are we?' Her intention was obvious – to take him back to their own time for treatment.

'I think you wore out your chances of getting him treated at your hospital last time we did this trick,' Adam warned her.

'That's true,' Helena agreed. Some time earlier they had managed to get Erimem's mentor Antranak treated in a modern hospital, but it had caused a lot of trouble and a mountain of paperwork.

'The computers in my home can make you anything you need,' Erimem offered. That was perfectly true. Her Habitat could be programmed to be anything they needed it to be.

A curious passenger peered out into the carnage of the corridor. Andy sent them back inside quickly. 'Just go back inside,' she barked. 'Everything will be all right.'

'Time to go,' Erimem said.

A moment later a roiling ball of electricity swept them away, leaving the corridor a shattered mess.

Erimem's villa crackled into existence around her group of friends as they materialised in the travel chamber.

Helena was immediately focused on her patient, who was being carried by Adam and Erimem. 'Okay, I'll tell you what I need the computers to synthesise...'

'No need,' Erimem interrupted. 'Andy and I have prepared for this.'

That confused Helena. 'You have?'

Erimem nodded. 'After Antranak was hurt and needed hospital treatment.'

'And we had to put up with all the shenanigans at the hospital with the police,' Andy added.

Erimem picked up the explanation again. 'So we decided to make sure that would not be a problem again.'

Mason had lost a lot of blood but had struggled back to consciousness. 'Where am I?'

'Don't ask,' Adam answered. 'We're getting you medical treatment.'

'You have to get the book,' Mason hissed. 'Don't let him get to England. He'll sell it at *Les Ambassadeurs* in London if he does. I heard that in the hotel room.' A surge of pain brought a grimace which Mason bit down on hard. 'Don't contact MI6,' he hissed, 'not unless you can get directly to the Chief. I don't know who I can trust.'

'How can you be sure you can trust us?' Erimem asked.

The answer came instantly. 'You didn't try to kill me and now you're helping me. I'd say you're my best bet at the moment.'

'We can't argue with that,' Helena said. 'But you need treatment now.'

Erimem led the way through to the main living area and ushered Andy to the discretely recessed computer panel on the wall.

After keying in few commands, Andy stepped aside. A door had appeared in the wall a few metres further along the wall. 'In there,' Andy said, pointing at the door.

Through the door was a full-size operating theatre, complete with a full staff of doctors and nurses, all scrubbed and prepared for surgery.

The nurses took Mason from Adam and Erimem and laid him on a table before beginning to cut his clothes away.

'Bad puncture wound,' Helena said. 'It's...'

'We're quite capable of taking it from here,' one of the surgeons said considerably more sharply than he needed to.

Helena's face scrunched into a horrified frown. 'Mr Robertson?'

'This fellow needs a surgeon, doesn't he?' the masked doctor boomed. 'Who else would they send for?'

'Well, in your mind, nobody,' Helena answered acidly.

'Out!' Mr Roberton barked. 'Out of my theatre!'

Helena was led out by Andy and Erimem. After the door closed, she looked at Andy, utterly bemused. 'You programmed a full operating theatre into this place?'

'Full ward, actually,' Andy answered, sounding thoroughly pleased with herself. 'The nurses are all really hot, too. I've had a thing about nurses ever since I saw *Carry On Doctor*. You can keep Barbara Windsor. I really fancied Anita Harris.' She held up her hands before Helena could object. 'Which doesn't matter here and now, I know.' She nodded back at the ward. 'They're all programmed with every bit of training a nurse gets, and a whole load besides. The Doctors have every bit of surgical knowledge on Earth programmed in, too.'

Helena was only partly placated. 'Did you *have* to make the surgeon old Grizzler Robertson?'

'Friend of yours?' Andy asked.

'In every possible way, no," Helena answered. 'He's rude, objectionable, arrogant.' She grimaced before adding reluctantly, 'Damn good surgeon, though.'

'Which is why the computers picked him,' Andy answered.

Helena finally conceded. 'All right. At least we know he'll be all right with that lot. Even though Robertson's a total arse of a man.'

That was Erimem's signal to return to their main task. 'Then we can leave Mason with them and go back to get the book.'

Before they could move, Adam held up his hand in confusion. He pointed at the hospital door. 'I know that isn't the door to the guest suite, but doesn't that hospital area fill the space the guest rooms would be in?'

'No,' Andy answered. 'The space inside this Habitat doesn't follow the same rules as space in our universe. You could have two doors side by side that both came out at the half way line of completely different football pitches.'

'That's absurd,' Adam muttered, 'but I say that a lot these days, so I'm just going to accept it and we can get on with things.'

Andy gave him a supportive punch to the arm. 'Smart move.'

Erimem was already thinking of their next move. 'Now we must decide where and when to intercept this criminal LeVal.'

'What's the next time and place we know he has to be at?' Adam asked.

'The port for the sailing of his ferry,' Andy answered.

Erimem nodded firmly. 'Then we should go there.'

Rene LeVal arrived at the port less than half an hour before boardings for the ferry were due to close. He was actually relieved to be cutting things so fine. He had left his pursuers behind, and if he had only just made it to the port on time, there was no chance that they would catch up with him.

At least there *should* be no chance of them catching up with him.

Rene had been in his business too long to take anything for granted.

He used his forged passport to board the ferry, offering his friendliest and most charming smile to the officials he dealt with. As far as they knew, he was just another tourist on his way to England.

Rene kept his eyes sharp as he made his way up to the various levels set aside for passengers to use on the journey. He scrutinised the faces in the bars and restaurants, seated in the lounges and browsing the shops in search of any familiar faces but he didn't recognise anyone. Moving to the large window looking down over the quay, Rene felt a slight jolt underfoot as the ship finally pulled away from its moorings.

A smile spread across his face as he looked down.

The odd-looking gang of four who had instigated all the trouble on the train were running towards the quayside. The look of frustration on all of their faces made him chuckle.

Even Rene would have to admit it was a rather unpleasant sound.

The journey by hovercraft was quick but noisy and it stank of diesel. The craft took far less time to cross the Channel than the ferry but the difference in departure times meant that Rene and the ferry would beat Erimem and her friends to England by more than an hour.

'We could just zap back to the villa then pop over and be waiting for buggerlugs,' Helena suggested.

Andy shook her head and scratched at her chin. 'I've been thinking about that,' she said. 'I think I know why we really missed the boat.'

'You cocked up the co-ordinates?' Adam suggested.

Andy shook her head. 'Nope. Space Grandad.'

'Why would he do that?' Helena frowned.

'To test us,' Andy said. 'See how we cope when things go wrong.'

'That sounds like him,' Erimem confirmed unhappily.

Helena snorted in frustration. 'He's a git, isn't he?'

'That also sounds like him,' Erimem agreed. She puffed her cheeks out and looked around the inside of the hovercraft. She was clearly not enjoying this journey at all. 'Can this thing go any faster?'

Adam gave her a worried look. 'You're not thinking of doing anything stupid like jumping from the hovercraft onto the ferry are you?'

'If it will get me off of this thing sooner I might,' she answered queasily.

Andy patted her arm sympathetically. 'Not loving it?'

'Not really,' Erimem answered. 'The movement and the smell.'

'Diesel,' Adam supplied.

Erimem nodded. 'That's it.'

'Yeah,' Andy agreed, sniffing the air and making a sour face. 'Strong, isn't it?'

Erimem sighed and tried hard not to throw up. 'There are times I really dislike my grandfather.'

'Amen to that,' Helena agreed.

Adam nodded. 'Yep.'

'Full house,' Andy muttered.

After arriving in England Rene LeVal again made sure that he was not being followed and made his way to the train station. He bought a one way ticket to London on the next available train.

Settled into his carriage, Rene looked with disdain at the dowdy middle aged woman opposite and at her grey husband. So these were what the French called "Les Rosbifs". This was what had stood against Hitler? How could a people with so much courage have so little style or flair? It didn't matter. What mattered was that he had made it to England and he was heading to London where he would sell that notebook and then he would have the life he had deserved for so long.

Erimem was almost green by the time the hovercraft finally disembarked. She decided it was not a good look for her.

They made they way to the train station. They had no way of knowing that they had missed Rene LeVal's train by just a few minutes.

Settling into their carriage they began to make plans – and Helena was making most of those plans.

'We need clothes,' Helena said.

Erimem pulled at the sleeve of the top she was wearing. 'We are wearing clothes.'

'And we are going to a proper 1960s gambling club,' Helena explained patiently. 'We need very particular clothes for a place like that. Trust me. I know the Sixties.'

'So what clothes do we need?' Erimem asked.

'And where do we get them?' Andy added.

Helena just grinned in reply.

'Carnaby Street?' Andy's face grew into a huge grin. '*Carnaby Street?*'

In the 1950s, Carnaby Street had been just another rather shabby backstreet in Soho, home to any kind of shop and business, from locksmiths to sweatshops to low-end tailors. However, as the grey post-war austerity of London started to give way to a world filled with rock'n'roll in the latter half of the decade, Carnaby Street began to play home to more interesting establishments, particularly John Stephens' boutique, *His Clothes*. That shop's success led to other fashionable clothes retailers moving in until, by the middle of the 1960s, Carnaby Street was *the* place to go for the most swinging, freshest fashions in London. Everybody shopped there, from Jimi Hendrix to the Beatles to Sean Connery. It helped that the legendary *Marquee Club* was just around the corner in Wardour Street and often hosted huge bands like the Rolling Stones, the Who and the Small Faces. The bands and their fans often shopped in Carnaby Street, which just added more prestige to the place. Mods, hippies and even the peacock movement all found just exactly what they wanted and a lot more on that fabulous street.

Andy looked all around at the impossibly vivid fashions, the daring make-up, the ridiculously short mini-skirts and absurdly-plastic-looking boots.

It. Was. Perfect.

'It's the cliché and better,' she said happily. 'Are we too early for Mary Quant?'

Helena's eyebrow lifted. 'Remember, we're too chesty for Mary Quant.'

'Damn these funbags.'

'Wasn't that a band from the Eighties?' Adam asked. 'The Funbags Three?'

'Funboy Three,' Helena corrected. 'Fun-*boy*.'

Andy gave a hearty laugh. 'If we have three, either solo or between us, something's gone very wrong.'

Adam shrugged. 'You haven't seen *Total Recall*, then.'

'Oh, fair point,' Andy nodded. 'She wore them well.'

'I wouldn't fancy having three.' Helena joined the discussion. 'Ruin the cut of my clothes.'

Andy agreed. 'Besides, two are annoying enough.'

Erimem frowned at each of them in turn. 'I have no idea what you are all talking about.'

'That's another on the list for movie night,' Adam said and then smiled at Erimem. 'We'll explain later.'

'So where are we going?' Andy asked Helena.

The older woman looked back and forth, drinking in the familiar sights. She looked incredibly pleased to be back. 'I know the very places.'

As it turned out, Helena *did* know exactly the best places to go in 1967 London to find a selection of appropriate clothes for the era... and for any situation they might expect to face.

They had more than four hours of shopping in the boutiques and exclusive clothes shops in the most fashionable parts of London. They bought more clothes than they were liable to need but thought it wise to cover every eventuality that might arise.

After an afternoon of shopping they took a suite of rooms at the *Commodore*, one of London's better kept secrets when it came to exclusive hotels.

'Even better than *Bertram's*,' Helena had promised. 'A much younger crowd.'

She proved to be correct, with *the Commodore* playing host to a number of well-known visitors to London. There were politicians, diplomats, actors and singers as well as minor members of Europe's old royal houses. Helena waved a greeting to two long-haired men heading into a lift. 'Eric. Ginger.'

The men smiled, gave a thumbs up and then disappeared from view as the lift doors slid closed.

'Long story,' was all Helena said in explanation.

The suite was perfectly Sixties, with "modern" plastic chairs and clear tables all shaped in designs that could only have come from the Sixties. The décor was undeniably of the period too, with bold geometric shapes in vivid colours.

'Groovy, baby,' Andy said. 'Totally shagadelic.'

'We have a few hours before we go out again,' Erimem said. 'We should get some sleep before we go.'

'Or we could go out and soak in the Swinging Sixties for a few hours,' Helena suggested.

Erimem conceded defeat and plucked a black and white dress from her shopping. 'Or we can enjoy the Sixties for a few hours.'

Les Ambassadeurs began its life as a private club for gentlemen in the seventeenth century. Membership had initially been reserved for the elite of London society but soon enough it had simply been enough to have money... a *lot* of money.

Over the decades and indeed the centuries, and often to the dismay of more staid, traditional patrons, the club had broadened its membership until just after the Great War, women had been allowed to entered this former bastion of masculinity, and after the Second World War financial reality forced the club's managing committee to admit day members... as long as those day members were willing to pay a hefty fee to hobnob with the great and the good.

At the end of the nineteenth century, the club had added a restaurant to its premises, hiring one of the finest chefs in the city to establish it as a prestigious location to eat straight from the outset. In the intervening seventy years only the most exceptional chefs in Europe had been allowed to run the kitchen, maintaining its reputation for excellence.

It was, however, the reputation of the gaming and gambling which kept the club alive and prospering. Everyone who enjoyed high stakes gambling knew that *Les Ambassadeurs* was the best place to go in London, both for its public tables and for the opportunity to arrange a private game.

It was also, rather contrarily, one of the places to be seen, and at the same time a location for illicit and clandestine encounters. These encounters could be personal or business, or both at the same time. The staff of the club would assure as much confidentiality as the customer required.

Despite being a weekday, *Les Ambassadeurs* had been busy when a party of four had arrived. A man in a black tie and evening suit was accompanied by three impeccably stylish young women. One in her early thirties had wavy black hair and wore a single shouldered teal green designer gown. A younger woman with a daring red flash in her short dark hair wore a high-necked dress in deep burgundy and the third woman, wore a midnight blue gown with seemed to shimmer as she moved, complementing her North African complexion, as did the impeccable Egyptian themed make up around her eyes.

'Okay,' Helena said as they moved through the casino, 'I'd say we've caught some attention.'

Speak for yourself,' Adam answered. 'There's not one pair of eyes in this place looking at me.'

'Other than the guys asking, "who's the dude with the three hot chicks?" maybe,' Andy offered.

Adam shook his head. 'Trust me, nobody's noticed the startlingly handsome young man with you three.'

'Damn, you're smooth,' Andy grinned. 'You could almost make me turn straight.'

Adam retuned the grin. 'No, I couldn't.'

Andy wrinkled her nose and enjoyed the banter. 'Nah. You're right. You couldn't. The dangly bit is off-putting.'

Helena leaned across and interjected. 'I don't think this is the kind of chat they're used to here, do you?'

'Sorry,' Andy conceded. 'I was forgetting what you said. "Be classy", wasn't it?'

'Something like that.'

As usual, Erimem's mind was focused on the task ahead of them. 'We should split and look around the casino.'

'You're right,' Helena agreed. She nudged Andy. 'Ms Hansen, would you care you join me?'

Andy adopted her most polished tone. 'Don't mind if I do, Dr Hadmani.'

Erimem led the way to a pillar at the side of the main gaming saloon. Thick, plush drapes all but hid the little corridor running round the outer edge of the room. Club staff used that passageway to move around the room unobtrusively. Erimem's party watched the magnificently dressed patrons sipping at drinks and enjoying the atmosphere as they moved from table to table. The air smelled of tobacco, alcohol and excitement.

'If nothing happens we will meet again back here in thirty minutes,' Erimem said.

Helena and Andy nodded and eased themselves away to the right. Erimem and Adam moved off to the left.

'Apparently there's something about the scent and sweat and smoke of a casino that are nauseating at three in the morning,' Andy said.

Helena looked at the clock on the wall. 'It's just gone nine. You're a bit early.'

Andy ignored her. 'Then there's quite likely the soul-erosion that's produced by high gambling...'

Helena interrupted, 'Which is, of course, a heady compost of greed and maybe fear and quite probably nervous tension – it like as not becomes intolerable or is it unbearable and the senses wake up and have a damned good revolt from it.' She sort-of finished the failed attempt at a quote and nodded. 'I've read the books, too.'

Andy looked around, feeling something dark land on her shoulders to begin pushing down on her joie de vivre. 'There's a sense of *something* here, isn't there.'

'Possibility,' Helena said. 'Anything could happen. Someone could become richer than Croesus or lose everything, all in the blink of an eye.'

Andy tried to lighten her mood again. 'Antici...' she held the pause several beats longer than she should before finishing, '...pation.'

Helena gave a wry smile. 'You're six or seven years early with that reference.'

'Don't tell me you saw the original Rocky Horror run.'

'More than once,' Helena confirmed. She led the way around the outside of the room, skirting the busiest areas and giving them a good view of what was happening.

'You should write your autobiography,' Andy suggested.

Helena shook her head ruefully. 'Who would believe it?'

'Fair point,' Andy conceded, eyeing a table where a card game was unfolding. 'Should we play a hand?'

'Not yet,' Helena said. 'We'd look gauche if we just went to a table and played without scoping the room first.'

That brought a smirk to Andy's face. 'Something tells me you have been to places like this before.'

Almost on cue, a tall young man with a noticeable chin and a very tall, very pretty, very ginger girl on his arm passed. 'Doctor,' he nodded. Helena just smiled in reply.

'What makes you think that?' she asked Andy as the young couple passed.

'Wild guess,' Andy answered glibly.

Helena sighed. 'I had to do something to pass the time until Ibrahim showed up.'

Andy surveyed the various tables. 'So, which of these games are you a winner at?'

'All of them,' Helena answered nonchalantly.

'I'm so glad we're friends,' Andy beamed. Borderline immoral misuse of time travel had already made all of the group of time travelling friends very wealthy, at least back in their own time. This was different, though. This was gambling in a casino in the Sixties.

Helena led Andy to a spot over by another pillar, from where they would see a well populated table. 'Let's take a moment over here, just to watch the room and keep an eye on the Baccarat.'

'Is that Burt Baccarat?' Andy asked.

'Shut up.'

Andy just smiled.

Erimem and Adam moved casually around the gaming saloon, exchanging smiles and nods with anyone they met, but they avoided getting into conversations. Adam looked around the crowd with a trained policeman's eye but for Erimem, studying the battlefield, searching for the enemy and observing them was all part of the training for war Antranak had given her.

She was always surprised at how easily her brain switched back to that mindset.

Adam's eyes were still on the crowd but there was some levity in his voice. 'I am definitely taking this suit back to our own time.'

'You look very handsome in it,' Erimem answered without shifting her eyes from the crowd.

'Don't I usually look handsome in my other clothes?' Adam asked playfully.

She still didn't look at him. 'I believe it is frowned upon to go in search of compliments quite so obviously.'

He squinted and watched an American lose a heavy bet. 'I thought I was being subtle.'

'No.'

Adam shrugged. 'That dress you're wearing is definitely coming home with us, too.'

'All of the clothes we bought are coming back with us,' Erimem answered. She continued to look across the room but saw nothing to demand her attention. 'We will leave nothing behind to say we were here.'

'Apart from chaos and mayhem?'

It was Erimem's turn to shrug. 'We cannot help those.'

Adam laughed quickly. 'Plus, they're fun?'

She risked looking away from the crowd for a moment. 'I am beginning to think you do not take time travel seriously,' she said, but she sounded indulgent rather than accusing.

Adam looked her in the eye. 'If it means I get to spend extra time with you I'm as serious as a heart attack,' he said sincerely.

There was something in the way he said those words that made Erimem feel... well, she wasn't sure exactly how to describe it but she was absolutely sure she liked it. 'Please do not have a heart attack,' was all she managed to muster in reply.

Adam didn't press it any further. 'Yeah, be hard to explain dying more than twenty years before I was born.'

That gave Erimem a chance to move the conversation to more comfortable ground. 'Your parents will be alive in this time period.'

'That's true. They'll still be kids at school just now.'

Erimem wondered what David and Fiona Docherty had been like as children. 'I like them.'

'Good,' Adam answered. 'So do I.'

'That is good to hear.'

There was just a hint of a pause before Adam spoke again, as if he was deciding whether or not to broach a subject. 'You talk about your father sometimes, but not as much as I would expect.'

It wasn't a matter Erimem talked about much. That part of her life was long in her past and so different from the life she lived now. 'That is a difficult subject for me to discuss. Most people cannot understand what our lives were like.'

'I suppose our backgrounds are quite different,' he answered wryly. 'The pharaoh and the copper.'

'Yes, they are,' she admitted. 'But, I hope, not *too* different.' That came out slightly more anxious than she had expected.

Adam had noticed that as well. 'I think we're doing okay.' He sounded confident and reassuring.

'I think this also,' Erimem said, 'But now is probably not the time to discuss that.'

'And you're probably right about that,' Adam agreed.

Erimem changed the subject of the conversation. She indicated the various tables. 'Do you know how to play these wagering games?'

Adam sort of scrunched his face uncertainly. 'I've been to casinos on a few nights out but a ticket for the Lottery is my usual flutter.'

Erimem digested the answer. 'We must try to look like we belong here.'

'The only people making any money here is the House,' Adam said. 'As long as we lose money we'll look like we belong.'

Erimem's eyebrows rose in surprise. 'You mean the gambling is not fair?'

'I mean that I've never seen a casino go broke, but plenty of their customers have.' There was no question about the inference in his words. 'The house always wins.'

Erimem wasn't too concerned about what that meant for them. 'Then we must lose money.'

'But not too much,' Adam warned. 'Nobody likes to lose too much.'

Erimem nodded. 'And we must keep our eyes alert for our prey.'

Adam started casting his gaze around the club again. 'He'll be here, sooner or later.'

'And so will whoever he intends to sell the book to,' Erimem said. 'We must look out for them, also.'

Adam's eyes were drawn to a dark-haired man who was also looking around the club, but it turned out he was simply looking for a young woman in a long red dress, who came up behind him and took his hand. 'It would help if we knew who they were,' he grumbled.

'That would be too easy,' Erimem said. 'My grandfather likes to make things challenging.'

That didn't improve Adam's mood. 'That's worrying.'

Erimem nudged his arm playfully. 'Don't worry. I will protect you from him.' She indicated the nearest table. 'Do you know this game?'

Adam nodded but looked far from enthusiastic. 'I'm terrible at it.'

Erimem's eyes had drifted from the cards. 'I do not think anyone will notice that.'

Adam was still looking at the cards. 'Why?' he asked.

'Look beyond the card table,' Erimem said.

There was no mistaking what – or more accurately who – Erimem was talking about.

A tall woman, perhaps in her mid-thirties had entered the saloon by some private entrance and made her way to the table they had been observing. She was tall, slim and wore a sparkling scarlet ankle length dress. Her long black wavy hair was impeccably styled so that it managed to be both wild and perfectly shaped at the same time. Her make-up, which suited her Mediterranean complexion, was bold and classic, her lips as vividly red as her dress. She wasn't fashionably thin in the mould of Twiggy and was more of a throwback to body shape more in vogue a decade earlier, but it was clear to everyone present that she did not care what fashion demanded. She was confident and in complete control of herself and her life.

Erimem recognised one other thing in this woman – she expected to be in complete control of *everyone* around her as well. It was clear in every movement she made.

Adam looked impressed by the woman's Hollywood style appearance. 'And I thought *we'd* made an effort.'

Erimem didn't take her eyes from this new arrival. 'Do you know who she is?'

'I haven't got a clue,' Adam answered.

'She is important, whoever she is,' Erimem said thoughtfully. 'She moves like a queen.'

'You would know,' Adam answered lightly.

But Erimem was not joking. 'And she moves like a lioness. She is a predator.'

'I don't doubt that at all,' he answered.

'I am serious, Adam.' Erimem's voice was sharper than she had intended, and she softened her tone as she continued. 'The way she moves… she gives the appearance of being relaxed, but her eyes are constantly watching.' She paused to let Adam observe the woman and see what she had already seen in her. 'She is always taking notice of everything around her. She knows where everyone in this room is and has already decided who is dangerous and who is not.'

'You're right,' Adam murmured. The humour had faded from his voice. 'Think she's worked out that you're dangerous?'

'I will be insulted if she has not,' Erimem answered flatly.

'So what do we do?' Adam asked.

Erimem took Adam's hand and led him towards the table at which this newcomer had seated herself. 'For now, we observe her. She seems to have chosen to play at a table. We will watch her and see what we can learn.'

The arrival of the woman in the red dress had been noticed by almost everyone in the room. Helena and Andy had seen her emerge from the passage behind the drapes before taking her seat.

'Eyes back on the room,' Helena said, nudging Andy's arm gently.

'My eyes *are* in the room,' Andy answered quickly. 'They're just scoping out Sophia Loren's sexier sister over there.'

Helena suppressed a smile. 'That's not a bad description of her actually.'

While happily married to her wife, Andy would readily admit that she could still appreciate the appearance of other women. 'She's got to be fifteen years older than me.' She shook her head. 'Her bra must be engineered by NASA.'

'Underwear in the fifties and sixties was more about torture than comfort,' Helena said with more than a hint of a bad memory coming back to haunt her. 'And leave Ms Loren Senior to Erimem and Adam. They're spotted her, too.'

'Spoilsport.' Andy playfully stuck her tongue out at Helena before beginning to look around the club again. 'Shall we drop some chips?'

Helena nodded. 'Why not?'

Andy's attention had been caught by a movement by the door. 'Wait a minute.'

'What?'

Andy nodded discretely towards the door. 'I spy with my little eye, something beginning with "scumbag".'

'What?' Helena turned and followed Andy's gaze.

'Our rabbit's just arrived,' Andy said quickly. 'He's over by the door looking about as comfortable as a nun in a knocking shop.'

It only took Helena a moment to catch sight of Rene LeVal. He was dressed in an evening suit which somehow managed to not fit him in any way at all. The trousers were just a little too long but the jacket's sleeves were just a bit too short showing just too much cuff on a shirt which was just that bit too loose around the neck. In a room filled with elegance, style and grace, he stood out like the sorest of sore thumbs.

'I see him,' Helena said quietly.

'Come on.' Andy started towards Rene, but Helena caught her arm.

'Wait.'

'Why?' Andy asked, but she didn't try to pull free. She trusted Helena completely.

Helena released her friend's arm. 'Let's see who he's trying to meet,' she suggested softly.

Andy frowned. 'That's not *really* our mission, is it?'

Helena gazed levelly at her friend. 'Right now, there's another me alive and at a party about two miles from here. If there are dangerous villains in the city, I want to find as much as I can to protect that earlier me.'

Andy understood Helena's reasoning. 'Because if anything happens to her…'

'…it won't be much fun for me,' Helena confirmed.

'Okay,' Andy agreed, 'let's see what he's up to.'

Discretely sticking to the edge of the room, the two women carefully eased their way towards Rene.

CHAPTER SIX

In the gaming room of *Les Ambassadeurs*, the startlingly beautiful woman in the shimmering red dress was the only topic of conversation. She had joined the Baccarat table and had immediately shown that her dominant personality extended to the card table. She played a hard, aggressive game.

As they moved around the table to find a better position to watch the game, Erimem and Adam heard snatches of various people's conversations about this mystery woman.

'Who is she?'

'Acts like she's the Queen of Sheba anyway.'

'Bit too pushy in how she plays for my liking.'

Finally they heard something of interest in a conversation between a sandy haired man in an evening suit and the young deb he was trying to impress.

'Xandra Caprice,' the young fellow said quietly. 'Some kind of European nobility. I saw her play in the Royale in France.'

'*That* was her?' The deb has clearly heard some chatter about the woman. 'I heard she took an English fellow to the cleaners and then took him to dinner.'

'Dinner in her suite apparently,' the fellow answered, and the girl giggled.

Erimem and Andy stopped listening after that. They had learned what they needed to learn and could leave the young couple to whatever their night would bring them.

They turned their attention to Xandra Caprice, just in time for the Croupier to name her as Banker.

'Miss Caprice takes the shoe.'

'*Principessa* Caprice,' the woman corrected immediately. She has a rich, velvet voice and spoke with a melodic Italian accent. A linguist might have recognised a hint of Neapolitan in her accent, though an expensive education had eradicated most of her background and left her simply sounding magnificently exotic.

'My apologies,' the Croupier said quickly. 'Principessa Caprice takes the shoe.'

Erimem watched Principessa Xandra Caprice as she dealt cards and gambled against the table's other players. The basics of the game were really rather basic. Players were dealt two cards and had to tally the closest to nine without going above that total. They could ask for an extra card in each hand but if they exceeded nine the game was lost. It took her a moment to realise that face cards counted as zero, but she filed that information and returned her attention to Xandra Caprice.

Long ago in the Pharaoh's Palace at Thebes she had watched gambling games being played out. She knew that whoever was in charge of the items used in the game usually had control of the situation. It was difficult to influence the outcome without being in contact with the dice or the table or the cards, or whatever else was being used.

Difficult but not impossible.

A gambler could also influence the minds of the other players around them, by making bold plays or holding a safety-first stance or just by bluffing. It quickly became very clear that Xandra Caprice played an aggressive, bold style of Baccarat which pushed many of the other players at the table to try to match her bravado. Erimem recognised the tactic. She had seen something very similar in battle many times. A general could gain an advantage by forcing the enemy armies to engage when it was not ideal for them to do so. She had watched her father and his general Antranak put enemies to the sword that way and had later used the tactic herself to bring a victory more than once.

Within half an hour of watching the woman play, Erimem knew that this Principessa Xandra Caprice was a very dangerous adversary indeed.

'She's almost wiped everybody out already,' Adam said softly.

'Yes,' Erimem agreed, mostly to herself.

It was true. Xandra had systematically worked her way around the table, targeting the weakest players and had hit them hard until they gave up or lost what little they had left, and then she moved on to the next weakest player.

There was one other thing Erimem noticed about Xandra Caprice.

The woman enjoyed beating her opponents. It had nothing to do with gaming or sport. She simply liked to show that she was superior to everyone else at the table. No. It was to prove that she was *better* than everyone else in the room, and the way she did that was by putting everyone else down and grinding her heel on them. Erimem had seen that sort of behaviour in her father's palace, too, but it had always been tempered by the knowledge that only Pharaoh had the ultimate power in Egypt.

Xandra Caprice seemed to believe that she had no-one above her.

Erimem realised one more thing about this Principessa Xandra Caprice, and that was that she disliked the woman intensely.

An older man with thinning, grey hair shook his head and threw up his hands as he lost to Xandra again. 'I know when I'm beaten. I will retreat from the field with a little honour still intact.'

'A wise move,' Xandra said. Her voice was deep but feminine and coated with velvet, but it didn't hide her disdain for her beaten opponent.

The old man moved away from the table and Xandra turned her head towards her next target but stopped as a shimmer of midnight blue moved into the defeated player's seat.

'I didn't think anyone else was going to join us,' she said.

'I enjoy a challenge,' Erimem said, sliding a large stack of plaques in various colours denoting different values onto the table.

'As do I,' Xandra Caprice answered, 'although there has been very little of that thus far tonight.'

'Well,' Erimem kept her face and voice completely neutral, 'the night is young.'

Xandra recognised the challenge and looked amused by it. 'And your name is?'

Erimem's bland answer gave away nothing. 'For my friends.'

The reply only seemed to amuse Xandra more. 'And we are not friends?'

'My friends don't try to take my money,' Erimem answered evenly.

Xandra's eyes strayed to the stack of plaques by Erimem's hand. 'You seem to have rather a lot of it.'

Erimem answered without missing a beat. 'And you seem to have rather a lot of other people's money.'

Xandra was looking at Erimem intently now. She hadn't been able to intimidate the younger woman and Erimem could see Xandra trying to work out exactly who she was. 'You are a very confident little girl.'

'And you show commendable nerve for one so old,' Erimem replied quickly.

'Old?' There was just the slightest hint of irritation in Xandra's eyes at Erimem's riposte. She hid it quickly but it had been there. 'I suppose to a child anyone over twenty five is old,' Xandra continued dismissively.

Erimem was waiting for a statement like that. 'And to one so old, anyone under thirty is a child.'

Yes, she had scored a little victory against Xandra Caprice there. She saw it in the Principessa's eyes. She had gained the woman's attention and baited her into becoming more aggressive.

'You talk well,' Xandra Caprice sneered, 'but do you have anything to back your bravado?'

Erimem calmly tapped her stack of plaques. 'This is not enough?'

'Not without courage,' Xandra answered.

Erimem met that face on. 'My courage in battle has never been questioned.'

That definitely caught Xandra's attention. 'Ah, you are a soldier.'

'A *warrior*,' Erimem corrected, and this time she allowed a little arrogance into her tone.

Xandra evidently caught the change in manner. 'And you seek to go to war with me?'

'My father was a far greater warrior than I,' Erimem said. 'More than once I heard him say that he would try to never start a fight, but he would always finish it.'

That made Xandra pause just for a moment, weighing the challenge and the young woman issuing it before answering. 'And what is it that *you* say?'

'I would say…' Erimem pursed her lips and then stared hard into Xandra's eyes. 'I believe the phrase is that "the cards are growing cold".'

'You have got to be shitting me,' Andy said.

'What?' Helena asked. She followed Andy's gaze and saw Erimem seated at an oval card table playing against the woman in red who had demanded to be called "Principessa Caprice". 'Tell me I'm seeing things. Has she ever played this game before?'

Andy gave Helena a disbelieving look. 'Are you kidding? She can't even play Snap.'

Losing the money didn't bother Helena but she was interested in knowing why Erimem would get involved in a game like this when they had such an important task at hand. However, she could hardly just go over and ask what the hell Erimem thought she was playing at. 'We'll have to trust that she knows what she's doing.'

'I will remind you that you said that,' Andy grumbled. 'Especially if it all goes Pete Tong.'

Helena just started to move away, ushering Andy to follow her. 'We have our own work to do.'

Andy took a few quick strides until she had caught up with her friend. 'Where is he?'

Helena already had her eyes on Rene, who was now talking to a painfully thin man. 'Over there. And who's that he's talking to?'

'Obviously I have no idea,' Andy answered, 'but I'd suggest a bit of eavesdropping might be in order.'

Helena liked the sound of that. 'How terribly clandestine of you.'

'I thought so,' Andy beamed, and opened her arm out inviting Helena to lead the way. 'After you.'

Before sitting at the gaming table, Erimem had been almost certain that Xandra Caprice was not cheating. She had played poker with her friends before and while the game had not interested her, the interplay at the table had been fascinating. She had also been intrigued that each of the people she was playing had some knowledge of how to cheat when playing card games, whether it was marking the cards with a thumbnail, placing a shiny surface on the table so that the dealer could read the cards being dealt or any one of a dozen other methods.

The fact was that Xandra Caprice was not, as far as Erimem could see, cheating at all.

That had encouraged her to sit and challenge the woman. It helped that the money at stake meant nothing to Erimem. If needs be she could simply get more.

She wanted to see how Xandra Caprice reacted when someone pushed back against her, and while she had no interest in playing cards, Erimem was confident enough to set her knowledge of tactics in battle against whatever experience the older woman had.

As play resumed, Xandra went back to her tactic of wearing down the weakest player until they were unable to continue and then moving to the next target. It soon became apparent that she was saving Erimem for last. It might have been thought that she was ignoring the younger woman except that every now and then, even when her concentration should have been focused on the player she was targeting, Xandra would glance at Erimem from the side of her eye. It was so brief that it was almost unnoticeable.

Almost.

Erimem had spotted those looks and she knew that she had made her way deep under the other woman's skin.

She allowed a small smile to tug at the corners of her mouth.

Rene LeVal had dreamed of a life of opulence and luxury. Throughout all of his long criminal career he had hoped that one day he would steal or scam enough to wind up in places like this. However, now that he was in *Les Ambassaeurs*, surrounded by the wealthy and the elite, Rene couldn't wait to complete his business and get out of the place. It all felt alien to him. He didn't move the way these people did. He didn't carry himself with the same arrogance and confidence they did. Somehow his clothes – expensive as they were – didn't seem to hang on him they way these people managed to wear them. He simply knew that he didn't belong there. And he was sure that everyone around knew that too.

Well, that didn't matter.

Soon enough he would have his money and he would be on his way. He would find his way to a hot little island in the Caribbean somewhere and live a quiet, comfortable life, enjoying the local drinks and the local women, and he would never have to work again.

'Monsieur?'

Rene looked up to see a pencil-thin man looking at him with condescending, dismissive eyes.

'Yes,' Rene confirmed.

The cadaverously thin man showed no emotion. 'You are here to meet with my employer.'

Rene didn't like the man's tone or manner and puffed his chest out in challenge. He hadn't backed down from the Nazis and he wouldn't be cowed by this walking corpse. 'I am here to meet with a number of people,' he said pompously.

'Quite so.' The thin man showed no emotion but indicated for Rene to follow him along the passage around the outer edge of the room. 'This way.'

Helena and Andy had managed to stand close enough to Rene during his conversation to hear what had been said but with the drapes stopping them from being seen.

'I wonder where they're going?' Andy asked.

Helena scrunched her nose and shrugged. 'Be rude not to find out, wouldn't it?'

'Absolutely,' Andy agreed.

As quietly and discretely as possible, the two women slipped behind the drapes and followed Rene and his contact.

It hadn't taken long for Xandra Caprice to despatch her final two long-standing opponents at the card table, and she was left facing only Erimem. The older woman now wore the contented expression of a cat ready to play with a mouse before devouring it.

Erimem, on the other hand, looked entirely untroubled by her opponent or her progress.

When Xandra's eyes fell on Erimem she had settled in to enjoy the inevitable victory.

Adam had leaned close to Erimem's ear. 'Are you sure you know what you're doing?' he whispered.

'Not really, no,' Erimem answered equally quietly, 'but sometimes it is better to act than to think.'

'I am definitely going to remind you that you said that,' Adam said, and stepped back from her chair.

The game had started slowly. Erimem gambled cautiously and duly lost modestly, though she seemed untroubled to have won only one hand from the first six she played against Xandra.

Before the seventh deal, Xandra suggested raising the stakes and Erimem agreed, and then lost twice more. Her lack of concern at losing consistently seemed to intrigue and disappoint Xandra.

One of the casino's employees eased into position at Xandra's shoulder and slipped a piece of paper in front of her. She gave no acknowledgement, and he faded back into the background.

Xandra quickly read the note and her nose twitched in irritation. 'Unfortunately, I must call a halt to tonight's... well, one can hardly call it competition. Let's call it "entertainment".'

Erimem had spent enough time observing Xandra to have some measure on the woman's character. She knew that only something of vital importance could drag the older woman away from the table. She decided that it was time to play seriously.

'Nothing important, I hope,' she said.

'No,' Xandra said casually. 'Some business has cropped up.'

That gave Erimem her opening move. 'Are you double booked?' she asked.

Xandra didn't react. 'Nothing so mundane.'

'You should be more careful,' Erimem said blandly. 'Perhaps you should keep track of things... maybe in a *little black book*.'

That certainly caught Xandra's attention. She stared hard at Erimem and there was no disguising the open challenge in the younger woman's eyes.

'Perhaps I should,' Xandra replied slowly. 'Do you know anything about little black books?'

Erimem slid her impassive mask back into place. 'I have an interest in one.'

'Do you indeed?' Xandra said softly.

Before the older woman could offer a riposte, Erimem needled her just a little more. 'They are very useful things, Miss Caprice.'

'*Principessa* Caprice,' Xandra answered sharply.

This time everyone could hear the annoyance and lack of control in her voice.

Erimem gave a short, rather dismissive laugh. '*Principessa.* I am sure that impresses in the provinces.'

That jibe certainly struck a nerve. Xandra Caprice's eyes widened in anger. 'And you are...?'

Erimem met the woman's gaze evenly. 'I do not wear this make-up for show,' she said. 'My family ruled the known world. I am heir to a line that stretches back thousands of years to the Pharaohs of the Two Kingdoms of Egypt.'

Xandra looked hard at Erimem and Erimem held the woman's eyes squarely and without flinching. She was telling the truth and very soon she could tell that Xandra Caprice believed her.

And that put Xandra on the back foot.

For the first time in a very long time, perhaps the first time in her life, Xandra was facing an opponent she could not intimidate.

For the first time she had a *real* challenge.

The question was how she would react to that.

'Suddenly you are much more interesting to me,' Xandra said thoughtfully.

Erimem glanced at the clock high on the wall. 'I am sure we both have other business to attend to. Shall we increase the stakes?'

Xandra still seemed uncertain of her opponent but tried to rally her composure. 'You have courage... or foolishness.'

'Life occasionally requires both,' Erimem answered nonchalantly before fixing her gaze on Xandra again. 'Do you possess either?'

That hit its mark, too. Xandra's eyes flared for a moment. 'I possess most of your money,' she answered sharply.

'And I would like it back.' Erimem pushed her entire stack of plaques into the middle of the table. 'Deal.'

Word of this confrontation had spread round the saloon and an impressive crowd had gathered. Xandra's destruction of the table had earned her few friends, and the room was entirely behind this calm young woman facing her. There were gasps and a rise in level on conversation when Erimem wagered her entire stack of plaques.

Xandra matched the bet and dealt the cards.

Erimem drew a ten and a five, giving her a total of five. It was a hand she had drawn three times before and each time she had played the sensible percentage game and played that five. It was a safe hand. Most gamblers would stick on that, and Xandra obviously expected her opponent to stick.

'Carte,' Erimem said.

Xandra's eyebrow lifted in surprise. 'Five is safe, my dear.'

Erimem's expression didn't waver. 'Life is not about being safe. *Carte.*'

Xandra slid a card from the shoe. She looked confident. Probability and chance were on her side.

A three.

Erimem now had a total of eight.

Xandra cursed and flipped over her cards. A five and a two. She had seven.

Erimem had won the hand and won back most of her money.

The croupier reached out to push the plaques towards Erimem but she held up a hand. 'Leave them there,' she said. 'If you have no objection,' she added to Xandra.

For the first time, Xandra Caprice looked genuinely surprised and not in complete control of the situation on the table. She quickly composed herself and nodded agreement. 'Of course. I enjoy a challenge.'

Xandra dealt again.

This time Erimem won by drawing an eight and a ten against Xandra's six and seven.

In two hands Erimem had regained her original stake and was up by several hundred pounds.

'Leave it,' she said again as the Croupier reached for the plaques.

The crowd's murmur grew louder.

And Xandra Caprice was unable to hide her growing anger. 'One more hand,' she said. She pushed her stack of plaques into the middle of the table. 'For everything.'

'Everything?' Erimem asked blandly.

'Everything,' Xandra snapped.

Erimem thought for a moment and then nodded her agreement. 'One more hand.'

Xandra began to slide the cards from the shoe. 'A real test of courage.' She stared hard at Erimem. 'And luck.'

Erimem ignored the accusation that she was nothing more than lucky and chose to needle Xandra further. 'Do you believe in luck, Principessa?'

Xandra didn't quite answer. 'Do you... Pharaoh?'

Erimem just tilted her head slightly. 'The cards will answer that.'

Xandra slid the final cards from the shoe. For herself she drew a pair of fours.

Eight.

The crowd rumbled unhappily. They didn't want to see Xandra win but an eight was hard to beat.

Erimem turned her cards over.

A queen.

A nine.

Xandra swore harshly in Italian.

Erimem had returned her expression to bland and impassive, all except for her eyes. They blazed with satisfaction. 'I believe a Pharaoh beats a Principessa.'

Xandra Caprice cursed again and swept away from the table. The crowd parted to avoid bearing the brunt of her fury, before a few offered congratulations to Erimem. She accepted the plaudits without taking her eyes from the receding figure of Xandra until she disappeared from sight through a doorway.

Adam tapped the Croupier's arm and indicated Erimem's winnings. 'Would you have those changed for the lady, please?'

The Croupier was happy to oblige. 'Of course, sir.'

The crowd around Erimem had dispersed and Adam gently eased to her side. 'How did you do that?'

'Do what?' Erimem asked innocently.

'Don't.' He glared at her. 'You know what I mean. How did you beat her? Was it some military tactic? Watching her for tells?' He waited impatiently.

Erimem shook her head. 'It was nothing like that.'

'How then?' Adam demanded.

Erimem thought for a moment and then sniffed casually. 'I cheated,' she admitted quietly.

That took Adam completely by surprise. 'You what?'

'Or I *will* cheat,' Erimem corrected herself. 'At some point in future I will have someone come here and arrange the cards so that they come out this way. Probably Andy. She is very good at being sneaky.'

A broad grin slowly spread across Adam face. 'That's brilliant,' he said. 'I mean, horribly dishonest but *brilliant*.'

Erimem's calm expression didn't match Adam's excitement. 'It was necessary,' she said coolly. 'I needed to know our enemy and now I have looked into her eyes.'

'And what do you think?' Adam asked.

Erimem paused thoughtfully. 'I think she will try to kill us before this night is out.'

'Oh, good,' Adam muttered. 'That'll be nice. Why is nobody ever pleased to see us?' He raised a hand to attract the attention of one of the staff who was carrying a tray of glasses. 'I need a drink.'

Erimem nodded. 'So do I.'

Helena and Andy had followed Rene and his guide at a discrete distance until they had gone through a door marked PRIVATE SALOON. An enormously muscular man, squeezed unsuccessfully into a suit that was just too small for him, stood guard on the door.

Andy eyed the wall of muscle for a moment. 'I'm not sure he's evolved enough to speak, but he still says "sod off" to me.'

'He's a NO ENTRY sign that would punch you in the teeth,' Helena agreed. With that she started towards the giant figure.

'Hey, where are you going?' Andy hissed.

Helena's movements had become erratic and unsteady. When she spoke, her voice had lost all of its usual poise and was equally trembling. 'Ooh,' she said drunkenly to the man mountain, 'there's only one reason a big hunky man like you is left outside.' She drunkenly tapped the side of her nose knowingly. 'There's a private game going on in there.' She gave a sozzled giggle. 'Though that could mean two different things.' She pointed at the door. 'Is there a private game in there? Chemin de Fer? Baccarat? Tiddly-Widdly-Winks? Hide the sausage?'

'Move on,' the gorilla said.

Helena feigned drunken outrage. 'So there *is* a game! I demand to be let in.'

'Move on,' the giant rumbled again, considerably less amenably than before – and the first time really hadn't been all that amenable to begin with, 'or you'll be moved on, out into the street.'

Helena gave a splendid performance of drunken outrage, struggling to force herself vaguely upright. 'I've hardly ever been so insulted.'

The giant shifted his footing to move towards Helena, which was Andy's cue to intervene. She hurried to her friend's side caught her arm, and started pulling her away. 'You'll have to forgive my friend,' she said over-politely. 'She doesn't get out much. Hardly ever drinks. The champagne has gone right to her head. Between you and me and the brick wall, there's plenty of room in there.'

'I heard that,' Helena slurred.

'Just my luck. Her brain's turned to mince but her hearing is perfect.'

Andy apologetic smile was met with a growl from the giant. 'Get her out of here.'

Andy started to steer Helena back the way they had come. 'Thank you for being so understanding,' she said to the guard. 'I'll just take her away and find a bucket to pour her in.'

'Ooh,' Helena grumbled unsteadily. 'I think I might need a bucket. I don't feel so good.'

'Take her away *quickly*,' the guard said hurriedly. He clearly did not want to deal with a drunk throwing up or the commotion it would cause.

'Come on, you old soak,' Andy said, helping Helena away from the guard and his door.

Andy led Helena back the way they had come. As soon as they turned the corner out of the guard's sight, Helena straightened up and dropped the drunk act. She gave her friend a very smug grin.

Andy just looked at her accusingly. 'You were too good at that.'

Helena shrugged. 'I've had practice over the centuries.'

That sounded like another hint of something that should go in Helena's memoirs, but Andy let it slide for the moment. 'So, was it worth being threatened by a shaved Yeti?'

Helena nodded, looking rather pleased with herself. 'I did see a few interesting things,' she said. 'I'm sure the room is almost soundproof – the door definitely is. The locks are primitive electronic, but the best this era has to offer. Oh, and Captain Caveman back there is neither observant nor bright, but he is carrying a Luger in a shoulder holster that hasn't been fit very well.' She tried to look modest but failed dismally. 'It shows through the clothes under his left arm which means he's right handed.'

'Check you out, Miss Marple,' Andy said, genuinely impressed. 'So there's definitely some kind of shenanigans going on in there.'

'Without a doubt,' Helena agreed, glancing back at the curve in the corridor which took the door and its guardian out of sight. 'Question is, how do we find out what it's all about?'

A woman's voice intruded from just along the corridor. 'I was thinking the same.' They turned in time to see the woman who had called herself Ilsa Lund step out from behind the heavy drapes. She was dressed in a very stylish black dress with a matching clutch bag in one hand… and a Baretta in the other. The pistol was aimed unerringly in their direction.

Andy sighed. 'Oh, bollocks.'

'Didn't we leave you in France?' Helena asked with forced politeness.

Ilsa indicated a door set into the outer wall of the corridor. 'In there.'

Andy shook her head and refused to move. 'She won't shoot us. There's no way she would get out without being caught. Everyone would hear the gun.'

Ilsa smiled and pulled a short black barrel shaped object from her bag and screwed it to the muzzle of her pistol. With the silencer now added, she wafted the pistol at the door again. 'Thank you for reminding me.'

Helena simply shook her head at Andy. 'Really?'

'Oh, arse,' Andy grumbled. 'Don't tell me – keep my big gob shut in future.'

Ilsa opened the door and beckoned again with the pistol, though far more menacingly this time. 'In.'

Erimem and Adam had retreated to a table away from the gambling and had obtained two glasses of a very fine champagne, gratefully provided courtesy of one of Xandra Caprice's earlier victims. The champagne Adam had requested from the staff would arrive just as they finished these glasses… at least that was their hope.

Adam was watching the room intently, waiting for events to unfold. 'What's the plan now?'

Erimem sipped slowly at her champagne. 'We will see what Helena and Andy have learned.'

Adam nodded at the reply. 'I can't see them anywhere.'

'Neither can I,' Erimem murmured, 'and that is usually a very bad sign.'

A bland, suited man approached their table and spoke quietly, in the deferential manner of one of the casino staff. 'Miss, your winnings are waiting for you in the manager's office.'

Adam looked mildly irritated. 'Why are they there?' he said. 'I asked for them to be…'

Erimem put a hand on Adam's arm and interrupted him. 'The money is not in the office,' she said.

Adam frowned. 'What?'

Erimem looked serenely, almost disdainfully, at the man standing by the table. 'This man does not work in this casino.' That deepened Adam's frown and his body language changed. He stiffened and his hands balled into fists. Erimem calmly continued to explain. 'The men here wear uniforms. The uniform shirts have letters embroidered on the cuffs and pockets. Their ties are of a similar colour but not of that material.'

Adam had scrutinised the suited man and looked annoyed for not spotting that he was an imposter sooner. 'You're right.' But he *had* noticed something. 'Those shoes. Would you say they look Italian?'

Erimem couldn't disagree. 'I have little expertise in men's shoes.'

'Trust me,' Adam said confidently. 'They're Italian.'

'As is Principessa Xandra Caprice,' Erimem noted mildly. 'I doubt if that is a coincidence.'

The fake casino employee put aside any pretence of deference. His body language changed, his back straightened, and his tone became harsh. 'Will this be easy or do things need to get unpleasant?'

Erimem was not in any way frightened of this man. 'You are here,' she said. 'That means they are already unpleasant.'

The fake employee did not react well to the insult. He opened his jacket to show a pistol in a holster. 'I will not kill you,' he said to Erimem before turning to Adam. 'I will kill *him*.'

Erimem looked back at the man and shook her head. 'You have made a very grave error.'

The man gripped the butt of his pistol. 'The only grave will be his, if you do not do as I say.'

Anger flared in Erimem's eyes and Adam saw it.

'Bad move, man,' he told their captor. 'Now she's annoyed.'

Erimem rose calmly to her feet and peered dismissively at the man who stood a head taller than her. 'Lead the way,' she said imperiously, 'or should I kill you here?'

The man shook is head at her confidence. 'She said you were arrogant.' He indicated for them to move. 'Go through the arched doorway.'

The doorway Helena and Andy had gone through led into a very comfortable room with couches and armchairs. There were no tables for gaming and Helena had suggested that it was a smoking room for members.

Ilsa Lund had not been impressed by the suggestion. In fact she simply hadn't acknowledged it at all and had instead indicted for Helena and Andy to move towards one of the couches.

'No disrespect,' Helena said, 'but I really hoped we wouldn't see you again.'

'And I really don't care what you hoped,' Ilsa answered. 'Where is Mason?

Helena looked at the classic Cartier watch she wore over her long gloves. 'He'll still be in surgery,' she said. 'You did quite a bit of internal damage to him.'

'That was the idea,' Ilsa answered sourly, before her lips pursed thoughtfully. 'So he's still alive? Pity. You must have moved him quickly.'

'We got him treatment in time,' Andy said. She smirked to herself and looked pleased with her pun.

Helena simply nodded her agreement. 'Literally.'

Ilsa had no idea of the secret meaning of their words. She was more interested in the pain she had caused Mason. 'The scars will give him something to remember me by.'

'And we're not asking what your history with him is,' Andy said.

'Because we're really not that interested,' Helena picked up from her friend. 'And it's not why you shoved us in here.'

'No.' Ilsa pushed the delightful thoughts of John Mason squirming in agony out of her mind and returned to business. 'And you are correct. I need to know where LeVal is.'

Andy didn't bother lying. 'He's behind the big door guarded by a bigger gorilla,' she said.

Ilsa seemed to have already suspected as much. 'Who else is in there?'

'No idea,' Andy answered.

Ilsa shook her head coldly. 'I don't believe you.'

Helena looked disappointed that she had to explain the situation to Ilsa. 'We were following him but couldn't get past the ape at the door,' she said as if she was talking to a rather dim child, 'and then there would be the trouble of the sound-proofed reinforced door with electronic locks.'

'Observant.' Ilsa was reluctantly impressed. 'Has he sold the book?'

'We don't know,' Andy answered.

'But probably not yet,' Helena added. 'Or he's currently in the process of doing so now,' she suggested. 'Which would explain the locked door and trained gorilla guarding it.

Ilsa nodded in agreement. 'That would also be my guess.' She aimed the Baretta straight at Helena's heart. 'And you would seem to have told me everything of value that you know.'

'What?' Andy blurted out. 'You're just going to shoot us now? After we told you all that? That's hardly fair.'

Ilsa simply shrugged. 'Life is rarely fair.'

'And I'd say you're rarely stupid,' Helena said confidently, 'so you won't kill us here.'

'Why not?' Ilsa seemed amused by the assertion.

'Because you're in here and what you need is in another room,' Helena said in that same *talking to a child* tone of voice, 'which we can get into but you can't.'

Andy only just bit off an incredulous "We can?"

Helena continued confidently. 'We reconnoitred the room for a reason but we burned the only chance he'll let anyone that close to do it.'

Ilsa looked unconvinced. 'So how do you plan to get in?'

A relaxed, assured smile spread across Helena's face. 'Sheer animal cunning and innate wit. I have a plan.'

'We're screwed,' Andy muttered.

'Quiet,' Helena said easily. 'No heckling from the cheap seats.' She stared confidently at Ilsa. 'I'll get us in there.'

Ilsa eyebrows rose sarcastically. 'And then you just hand the book to me?'

Helena shook her head. 'You wouldn't believe me if I told you that.'

'I wouldn't believe you if you told me water is wet,' Ilsa answered sharply.

There was bite in Helena's answer. 'So you have to decide if you want to get in there or if you want to distrust me and make snarky comments about it.'

Ilsa mulled the situation. 'I'll kill you once I have the book. You know that.'

Helena was unconcerned. 'And I'll try to stop you getting the book. You know that.'

'I would be disappointed if you didn't try.' Ilsa finally nodded, accepting the unavoidable need to have these two irritating adversaries to help her. 'Get me in there.'

Helena nodded. 'All right.'

Ilsa backed towards the door. She kept her pistol aimed steadily at Helena's stomach. She softly opened the door a crack. She glanced quickly into the corridor where she saw Erimem and Adam being urged in the direction of the private saloon's door by a man holding a Luger.

'Well,' Ilsa murmured, 'this got a bit more interesting.'

CHAPTER SEVEN

'Ah, *Pharaoh*.' Principessa Xandra Caprice drew deeply on her long, slim, black cigarette and looked across the table as Erimem and Adam were brought into the private gaming room. The table had chairs set for six players but Xandra was the only person seated.

The room was comfortably spacious without being large, perhaps twenty five feet by fifteen. The gaming table dominated the area but there were comfortable chairs against the walls, one of which had a friendly open fire crackling welcomingly. A muscular goon stood as sentry inside each of the two doors and another was positioned to the side of the leather couch in which Rene LeVal was perched. A cadaverously thin man stood nearby, his eyes always flicking to Xandra Caprice, waiting for instructions.

Erimem remained entirely untroubled by her situation. 'If you wanted a rematch, Principessa, you only had to ask politely.'

In private, with the doors closed, Xandra Caprice didn't bother with any further verbal jousting. 'I think we are past the time for games, don't you?'

'I recognise her,' Rene said, pointing at Erimem. 'Yes, I recognise her.'

One of Xandra's perfectly shaped eyebrows rose quizzically. 'From where?'

'She was in the fight in the hotel in Brussels,' Rene said, 'and then she was on the train.' His head bobbed in an animated nod. 'She missed the ferry to England.'

'That was careless of her,' Xandra said humourlessly, looking at Erimem with distaste. 'It was also careless to talk about a book you don't possess.'

Erimem was unconcerned. She let her eyes wander leisurely around the little saloon. 'Or was it careless of you to bring me into a room where that book is being kept.'

Her captive's lack of fear seemed to irritate Xandra. 'What makes you think it is here?'

Erimem nodded nonchalantly in Rene's direction. 'He would not still be here if you already had the book. He would either be paid off and running away...'

'...or lying dead in an alley,' Adam finished for her. 'My money's on my idea.'

The suggestion that his life might be in danger startled Rene. 'What? She would not do that. We have *un accord*. An agreement.'

'Okay,' Adam sighed. 'He wins the award for the stupidest thing anybody's said today – and given the kind of day we've had, that's quite the achievement.'

'You are wrong,' Rene protested. 'I will be paid.' He looked towards Xandra. The mixture of hope and desperation in his face was quite pathetic.

'After you hand over the book,' Xandra told Rene coolly.

Rene might have been desperate, but he was not completely stupid, and he held his ground. 'After I see the money,' he said.

However, it was clear that Xandra Caprice was in no mood to trade words with Rene. She looked at the cadaverously thin man standing beside the couch. 'Vincente?'

The man named Vincente indicated for one of the men standing inside the doors to join him. Between them they hauled Rene to his feet and the guard wrenched the Belgian's arm up his back.

'What are you doing?' Rene screamed in pain. 'Stop! Stop that! Please!'

The two thugs ignored his pleas and his begging was reduced to screams as the torture threatened to rip bone and muscle apart.

Adam had no affection for Rene, but this kind of brutality was beyond anything he could just accept. 'Is that really necessary?'

Neither Rene's screams nor Adam's protests concerned Xandra. 'I asked him to give me the book,' she said in a matter-of-fact voice.

'He doesn't have it!' Adam snapped angrily.

Erimem nodded her agreement. 'He would have to be very stupid to bring it in here while he negotiated for it.'

Adam nudged her arm. 'He *is* quite stupid though.'

'No,' Erimem shook her head but gave no other reaction as Rene screamed again. 'I think he has some cunning.'

Xandra had listened to the little exchange and turned to Rene, indicating for his torment to stop. 'So, you were smart enough not to bring the book here.' She paused to relish what came next. 'That does mean I will have to torture you to get its location.'

From somewhere deep I his past, Renen found a vestige of the man who took a stand against the Nazis and their threats. 'They can do what they want. I won't tell you.'

But Xandra Caprice just laughed at his show of bravado. '*They* won't do anything,' she purred. 'Why would I let them have the fun?' She opened a cigarette case. 'Do you smoke?'

'Of course,' Rene answered.

Xandra plucked a cigarette from the case. 'Bring a light,' she instructed. The man guarding the second door moved to do as she ordered.

'What are you going to do to him?' Erimem asked calmly.

Adam was more animated in his protest. 'Look, he's a scumbag but you can't just burn him.'

'Burn him?' Xandra laughed. 'That would be so... ordinary and mundane.' She held the cigarette out towards Rene. 'Try one of mine – a special blend.' As the cigarette came close to Rene's lips she abruptly snapped at the point where the tobacco should meet the filter and blew sharply on the broken section. A fine dust flew into Rene's face.

'What?' The Belgian tried to pull away but was firm firmly in place by Xandra's goons.

'What was that?' Erimem asked.

Xandra looked very pleased with herself. 'A little something to make him more helpful.'

Rene was blinking hard, apparently struggling to focus his vision. A sheen of sweat had already appeared on his forehead. 'What does that mean?' he yelled. 'What did you do to me?'

Xandra glanced at the large clock on the wall and make a show of counting the seconds. 'You will find out any moment… now?'

On cue, Rene screamed again, but this time it came from a mixture of fear and pain. He desperately tried to break free of the men holding him. At Xandra's instruction they let Rene go and he crumpled to the floor, slapping hard on his arms and trying to roll over on them to cover them. 'No. Stop it. Put it out. Help me put it out.'

'Does it hurt?' Xandra asked, without a hint of genuine sympathy. 'I imagine it really does.'

'What is it?' Erimem asked. 'What is happening to him?'

'It is your friend's fault,' Xandra answered lazily. 'He said I would burn him.'

Adam's work with the police had exposed him to enough people dealing with illegal substances. 'Now he thinks he's on fire. It's a hallucinogenic drug.'

Xandra nodded. 'Very fast acting and very effective,' she said approvingly, 'and it will make Mr LeVal tell me what I want to know.'

Rene screamed again and began clawing at the skin on his arms. 'Help me!'

'And you'll leg it without paying him,' Adam snarled at Xandra.

She was unmoved by the display of rage. 'When the legs are as perfect as mine, it makes sense to use them, little boy.'

Her reply only made Adam angrier. 'Little boy?'

Xandra still seemed amused. 'With a big ego.'

'Amongst other things,' Adam snapped.

Erimem poked him on the ribs. 'Are you flirting with her?'

Adam shrugged defensively. 'You know I prefer older women.'

'Older,' Erimem conceded, 'but not actually *old*.'

'Insulting child.' Xandra took half a step towards Erimem, ready to strike her, but brought her temper under control.

Adam smirked at how easily he had triggered Xandra Caprice's anger. 'She's older than she looks,' he said, looking at Erimem. 'Wears it well, though.'

'Thank you,' Erimem said affectionately.

'You are trying to distract me,' Xandra said. Whether that was true or not, she had lost interest in Erimem and Adam for the moment. Rene was a far more pressing order of business. 'But our screeching friend is more interesting.'

And Rene *was* still screaming. In his mind all he could see were the intense flames engulfing his arms, burning and charring the skin. He screamed as the pain seared through him and nothing he did could stop the fire. 'Help me! Help me, I'm burning!'

Xandra moved an old-fashioned wooden chair to a few feet from Rene and sat in it. 'Listen to me,' she said evenly. 'Listen very carefully to me.'

'Make it stop!' Rene shrieked.

'Then listen to me,' Xandra repeated. 'Listen. I can stop the burning but only if you tell me where the book is.'

Greed gave Rene the resolve he needed to refuse. 'No!'

Xandra drew another cigarette from her case. 'Tell me where the book is and this will stop.'

Rene whined but didn't give in. 'You're lying.'

'I can make the fires worse.' Xandra put the cigarette to her lips. 'All I have to do is raise my hand.' As she spoke she raised a silver lighter and pressed her thumb to light it.

Rene screamed in terror at the sight of the flame. 'No. Stop. Stop it! Stop it!'

Xandra moved the lighter closer to Rene's face. He couldn't move his eyes from the flame. 'Then tell me where the book is.'

She pushed it closer.

Closer.

Closer.

He couldn't control his terror any longer.

Rene LeVal's resistance broke.

'The casino,' he whimpered.

Xandra didn't withdraw the lighter. 'This casino?' Xandra demanded. '*Les Ambassadeurs*?'

'Yes.'

'Where?' Xandra edged the lighter a few inches closer.

Rene tried to push himself away but a couch and Xandra's thugs blocked his way. 'The casino,' was all he could say. 'In the casino.'

'Where?' Xandra roared, pushing the flame to just an inch from his face.

'The casino!'

'*Where* in the casino?' Xandra thundered.

There were tears in Rene's eyes. 'I put it in the casino! Make it stop!'

'Not until you tell me where the book is,' Xandra shouted.

But Rene was now past being able to give a better answer. 'It's in the casino,' he whimpered again, his voice tailing off. 'The casino. The casino.'

'He is useless.' Xandra threw the lighter at Rene and turned to the two thugs who had guarded the doors. 'Find the book. Find it.'

Adam's anger at Rene's torture had now turned to sympathy for the Belgian, who was still squirming in torment. 'Help him,' he demanded. 'Give him something. You must have an antidote.'

The idea left Xandra genuinely bemused. 'Why in the world would I have that?'

Rene still writhed on the floor. 'Stop it. Please. Do something. It hurts so much.'

Xandra laughed maliciously at his suffering. 'Well, London can be terribly cold. Leave him.'

Adam ignored the presence of Xandra's thugs and strode towards Rene. 'I'll help him.'

The Belgian had pushed himself up on one arm. Adam didn't break stride. He balled his right hand into a fist and slammed it hard into Rene's jaw.

Rene dropped hard to the floor, unconscious.

Adam wrung his fist and winced. 'Shit, that hurt.'

Xandra was disappointed that Rene's suffering had been brought to an end. 'At least he's quiet now, I suppose,' she said sourly before looking at Erimem. 'Now you can tell me what you know about the book.'

'That it does not belong to you,' Erimem said flatly before nodding towards Rene, 'or to him. It must be returned to its rightful owner.'

'Darling, I'm *stealing* it,' Xandra cooed in her most condescending voice. 'That makes me its rightful owner.'

'No,' Erimem snapped, 'that simply makes you a petty thief with a small title.'

That jibe struck home. 'And for your grand title you will still be as dead as the pharaohs,' Xandra snapped back.

'But not as dead as your soul,' Erimem answered.

That made Xandra laugh out loud. A genuine, hearty laugh. 'Darling little girl, I don't *need* a soul. I have *money*.'

A sly smile tugged at Erimem's mouth. 'But you don't have the book.'

'I will,' Xandra said confidently. She looked at her two muscular thugs. 'You two. I told you to go and find it. Tear the place apart if you have to.'

Erimem tutted and shook her head. 'The owners will not like it if you do that.'

Xandra threw her hands up dismissively. 'Then I will buy the club.' She jerked her head towards the door. 'Go.'

'Yes, Principessa.' The pair of thugs accepted their orders and headed for the door.

* * * * *

Ilsa Lund, with her Baretta still aimed at Helena and Andy, had just reached the curve in the corridor bringing the private saloon's door into view when the door opened, and two muscular goons emerged. Ilsa put out a hand to stop the other two women. 'Wait.'

The three goons grunted at each other – which seemed to be their first language – and the two from the private saloon moved away along the corridor, unfortunately in the same direction where Helena, Andy and Ilsa were pressing themselves against the walls.

'Where are they going?' Ilsa asked.

Helena and Andy were spared the need to admit they didn't know when Vincente, Xandra Caprice's skeletal sidekick, opened the door and spoke.

'Find the book,' Vincente said. 'Search everyone if you have to.'

'Yes, sir,' the thug grunted.

'Not you,' Vincente sniped. 'You stay on guard.'

'Yes, sir.'

The other two heavies were still in hearing rage and Vincente spoke loudly to them. 'I was talking to them. You heard the Principessa. Tear the place apart if you must.'

The door closed and the sentry returned to his watch.

The group of three women had taken advantage of Vincente's distraction to drop back around the curve in the corridor.

'They don't have the book,' Helena said quietly.

Ilsa raised her Baretta. 'Suddenly you are of much less use to me.'

'Oh, shut up,' Andy said irritably. 'I'm getting really tired of you waving that thing at me.' She looked to Helena for support, but Helena's gaze was on the pair of men mountains lumbering back around the corner.

'Excuse me, you enormous lump of muscle,' Helena said politely.

The nearest goon scowled. 'What?'

'I believe you're looking for a book?' Helena smiled.

'Uh?' It took a moment to register exactly what she had said. 'Where is it?'

Helena flapped her hands about, acting flustered. 'Well, I couldn't possibly tell you that, not on a first date. I mean, what would my mother think, what with me being a mere, weak woman and all...'

The thug grunted as Ilsa brought the butt of her Baretta down on the back of his neck – and it had absolutely no effect other than to make him look even more annoyed than usual. He became even more angry when his colleague crumpled to the floor revealing Andy standing behind him holding a metal stand, which normally had a restraining rope hooked to it.

'If you're going to hit a neck like that hit it with something bigger that your pop gun,' she told Ilsa.

The heavy began to turn, squaring up to these new adversaries... and then he stopped, stock still and completely immobile. For the first time he looked confused and afraid.

Helena came around his side, never moving the three fingers she had jammed into his shoulder and neck. 'Don't go anywhere yet. We need a chat with you.'

'Let go,' the thug wheezed. 'I can't breathe.'

'I know,' Helena said patiently, 'I'm a doctor. I spent long enough studying the human body to know how to make it stop working very easily. And you just about count as human.' She sniffed. 'I think.'

Ilsa looked at the frozen heavy in shock. 'He can't move.'

'I know,' Helena nodded cheerfully. 'Paralysis from a pressure point. Learned it in Tibet from an absolutely charming monk. He was an incorrigible cheat at cards, by the way. He would have loved this place.'

'Letting all the secrets out today, aren't you?' Andy laughed.

Helena smiled tightly. 'Can we come back to that when I'm not killing Guy the Gorilla here?'

'Sorry,' Andy said. 'My bad.'

'So,' Helena said to her victim, 'where is the book?'

With no chance of escape, the goon made probably the smartest decision of his life and told the truth. 'In the casino. We don't know where.'

'So you're searching the casino for the book?' Andy asked.

The goon didn't reply straight away, and Helena applied a little more pressure to his neck, causing him to gasp.

'Answer her,' Helena hissed.

'Yes,' the thug forced out.

'There. That's better,' Helena said. 'Nighty-night.' She twisted her fingers in his neck and the thug dropped noisily to the floor.

Ilsa looked surprised, and unexpectedly impressed. 'You did prove useful after all.' She raised her Baretta again. 'Pity I have to kill you now.'

They were saved by the arrival of the enormous goon who had been guarding the door. The sound of his colleague hitting the floor had attracted his attention.

'Hey. Who are you?' He saw Helena and Andy. 'Oh, you two again.'

Both Helena and Andy pointed instantly at Ilsa. 'Not us – her!'

The heavy saw the pistol in Ilsa's hand and lumbered towards her. Aware that she had no time to get a shot off, Ilsa threw herself at the advancing thug.

Erimem held up an imperious hand to stop Xandra's latest insult. 'Did you hear something from outside?' she frowned.

Adam shook her head and tilted his head to listen.

'I doubt it,' Xandra said. 'This room is sound-proofed. Privacy is very important in these establishments.'

Erimem ignored her statement. 'I definitely heard something.'

Adam nodded. 'So did I.'

Erimem pursed her lips. 'It sounded like…'

She didn't have time to finish before the something enormous crashed against the door, and it splintered inwards. It only took an instant to see that it was the goon who had been standing guard that had crashed through the door, head first. Someone was on his back, trying to choke him out.

'Jesus!' Adam yelped, pulling Erimem away from flying shards of the broken door.

It only took Erimem a moment to recognise the blonde woman on the thug's back. 'Her again?'

'Forget her!' Andy shouted, poking her head round the door. 'Bigger problems to deal with.'

Adam started pulling Erimem towards the door while Ilsa and the thug tussled on the ground.

Erimem glared back at Xandra Caprice. 'You are a lucky woman.'

Xandra looked furious but couldn't let Erimem have the last word. 'Always.'

Erimem looked set to throw another jibe but both Adam and Andy dragged her out through the door.

'Be witty later,' Adam urged. 'Come on.'

Erimem look relieved that Helena was also present and unharmed. 'The notebook is in the casino somewhere.'

'Oh.' Helena was slightly deflated. 'That was our news, too.'

'We need to find it,' Erimem said, leading the way along the corridor.

'Before Lady Muck's goons get it,' Adam added.

'Two of them are out of the picture,' Andy said, just as they reached the unconscious thugs.

'So I see,' Erimem noted, stepping over one of the heavies.

Andy pointed at one of the unconscious men. 'Helena accidentally beat him up.'

'I did a bit,' Helena admitted, and then poked the other man with the toe of her very expensive shoe. 'But Andy belted this one on purpose.'

'I am impressed,' Erimem said before turning and striding away along the passage.

The others hurried after her.

'She's impressed,' Adam said, 'but the pair of you scare the shit out of me.'

They caught up with Erimem in the main gambling saloon. She was looking around. They could almost hear her brain whirring. 'Where can he have hidden the book?' she asked.

'There can't be too many options,' Helena said.

Andy agreed. 'We saw him when he came into the main saloon. There was no sign of it there.'

Helena nodded. 'And we followed him from there to the private room.'

Erimem sucked her lower lip thoughtfully. 'And you did not see him hide the book?'

Helena shook her head. 'Nope.'

Andy agreed. 'I mean, he wasn't in sight every single second but I'm pretty sure Skeletor or any of the other henchmen would have spotted if he'd done something with it.'

Helena raised an eyebrow. 'Unless he was busy henching. You know how these henchmen get with their henching.'

Andy scowled at her friend. 'Okay, I won't use the word "henchmen" again.'

'And back on topic?' Adam urged. 'That means he hid it very quickly inside the saloon or stashed it somewhere outside before coming in.'

Andy frowned and tried to remember entering the club. 'What's outside?'

Erimem was already on her way out into the reception area. 'There is one way to find out.'

They hurried after her and found themselves in the rather dull and uninteresting reception they had come through an hour earlier. It was clean, neat and well-appointed but utterly unmemorable, and had nothing to encourage patrons to linger there when they could be eating, drinking or more likely, gambling. A few doors were marked with signs reading RESTAURANT, MEMBERS' LOUNGE, GAMING SALOON and various others, while there was a contained desk for checking coats and another for checking memberships. Large ferns jutted from old urns while sculpted bronze figures stood in reliefs in the wall.

'Could be in any of the plants pots,' Andy suggested, 'or stuffed behind statues...'

'We better check,' Helena said firmly.

Adam's eyes had focused on a desk where a rather snooty woman was giving instructions for how her precious fur coat should be treated. 'Or... you don't think he'd be stupid enough to just use the coat check, do you?'

'That would be very foolish,' Erimem said uncertainly.

Andy wasn't ready to dismiss the idea simply because it would mean Rene had made a bad decision. 'This is a guy who has stolen from a spy, double-crossed the local gangster, scammed a dodgy banker and then tried to do a deal with Whatsername in there – all in one day.'

Erimem could not argue with that logic. 'That is all true,' she said. 'You and Helena search here. We will see if he left a coat.'

Andy tugged her forelock sarcastically. 'Yes, Your Queenieness.'

Adam hiked a thumb back towards the gambling saloon. 'She's less pushy than Alotta Fagina back there.'

Erimem just frowned. 'That is not her name.'

'Another pop culture gap we need to fill in,' Adam said sadly. 'Austin Powers trilogy. Next movie night.'

'Oh, *behave*.' Andy grinned. 'On your way.'

Erimem and Adam began to move towards the coat check. 'We'll shout if we see Lexa Kimbo show up,' Adam called.

'Good name,' Andy muttered. 'I'm remembering that to insult people with.' As she and Helena moved away she was sure she heard Adam's voice say "Groovy, baby!".

The foyer of *Les Ambassadeurs* proved to be quite a bit grander and considerably larger than either Andy or Helena had anticipated. There was a small bar to the side which was exclusively for permanent gentlemen members, a last concession to the club's past and its more conservative members. Though they were unable to enter the room, Helena and Andy did ascertain that Rene had not been in there either. In fact, the only people they could see inside were two ancient, bearded gents who looked as if they had been there since before Franz Ferdinand had come a cropper in the Balkans. Their newspapers looked to be of similar vintage. They looked like they might just enjoy old news better than anything contemporary.

Another pair of old buffers sat in comfortable armchairs in front of a blazing fire in a little snug, discussing cricket and looked horrified as the two women peeked in before returning their attention to the relative strengths and weaknesses of Colin Cowdrey and Tom Graveney's cover drives.

'This is turning into a pain in the bum,' Helena muttered.

Andy agreed. 'We'll have to look in every nook and cranny.'

'Yeah, 'fraid so,' Helena nodded. 'I hope Erimem and Adam are having more luck.'

'I wouldn't bet on it,' Andy muttered and nodded her head in the direction of the coat check booth where Adam was having little success despite showing his police ID. Perhaps not surprisingly given that the ID came from more than fifty years later.

Adam was sighing in exasperation as the snooty attendant at the coat check counter gave him short shrift... and then the attendant disappeared backwards. His feet flashed into view for a moment as he was yanked out of view. A second later, Erimem stood in his place and was beckoning Adam towards a little door to the side. He quickly disappeared through the door into the booth.

'Do we add breaking and entering to her list of talents?' Andy asked.

'She might have picked that up from hanging about with us,' Helena said.

'I do hope so,' Andy grinned. I like being a bad influence. Still, we'd better get on with our side of things.'

Helena agreed. 'Let's think logically. If he came in the door which way would he go in search of a secure place to stash something valuable?'

They looked back at the front door and the various potential routes that might have appealed to a desperate Rene LeVal.

'Secure but easy to access if he had make a run for it...' Andy said, leading the way back to the door.

Helena walked slowly away from the door, as she imagined Rene would have done. 'So he comes in this way and looks around.' She glanced to the left where there was an alcove but with nothing inside it. 'Nothing over there.'

Andy pointed in the opposite direction where they had already searched. 'Old codgers in the comfy seats, and he didn't go into Misogyny Central.'

That left just one direction for them to search, the area with potted plants, art and statues.

'So this way?' Andy continued. 'Behind a painting?'

Helena shook her head, dismissing the idea. 'Too noticeable when he's doing it.'

Andy couldn't argue with that. 'Plant pot?' she suggested.

Helena looked unsure about that, too. 'Would he risk putting it in damp soil?' she asked. 'Worth checking, though.'

As discretely as possible, Andy checked inside the plant pots and stand. 'Nothing.' Her eyes fell on the statue of a naked three armed woman dealing cards. 'On the other hand...'

'Witty...' Helena said approvingly, 'and I see what you mean. That's a very appealing gap under the statue.'

'Isn't it just?' Andy agreed. 'You want to do the honours?'

'No, no,' Helena said. 'Your spot, not mine. Help yourself.'

Andy slid her hand under that statue. 'Nothing,' she said, the smile sliding from her face. But then, a very smug expression took over. 'Wait a minute. She withdrew her hand – and grasped in it was a small black notebook.

'Well, look at that,' Helena said. 'Aren't we clever?'

'Aren't you just?' A woman's voice said in a rich Italian accent.

Xandra Caprice and Ilsa Lund were standing a few yards away. Ilsa had her Baretta aimed at Andy. The club's patrons were backing away in alarm.

'Why is there always a buzz kill?' Andy sighed miserably.

'Give us the book,' Ilsa demanded.

Helena's eyebrow lifted with curiosity. 'Us?'

Ilsa nodded. 'The Principessa and I have reached an agreement.'

Helena snorted derisively. 'She bought you off.'

'I am not for sale,' Ilsa retorted angrily.

Helena didn't back down. 'But I'd guess you are for rent.'

'And you are stalling,' Principessa Xandra Caprice said. 'Give me the book or we will simply kill you and take it.'

Andy shook her head, looking at the dozen or so patrons watching this abuse of their club with varying amounts of fear, concern and sobriety. 'You're not going to just murder us here in front of all these witnesses.'

'Oh, don't worry,' Xandra said easily. 'We will kill them as well.'

Helena looked hard into Xandra's eyes. 'You'd enjoy it as well, wouldn't you?'

'Don't you have a saying in English about people enjoying their work?' Ilsa asked. 'Now give us the book.'

Andy handed the book to Helena. 'Do it. The police are almost here anyway.'

Xandra was becoming irritated by their stalling. 'I have played enough cards to recognise a bluff. The book. Now.'

Andy glanced at Helena and then shrugged.

Helena held out the book towards Xandra, who plucked it triumphantly from her grasp. 'Thank you.' She opened the book and flipped through its pages. Her eyes widened in surprise and delight. 'Whoever wrote this has been a *very wicked boy*. People are going to pay me a great deal of money because of the information in this book.'

Andy shrugged. 'Like we said, the police are nearly here.'

Xandra glanced down at the pistol in Ilsa's hand. 'Do you think we ae afraid of the police?'

Any further quip was cut off as a heavy overcoat was thrown over Xandra's head. Ilsa had time to register what was happening to her new employer before she also disappeared under a heavy overcoat. Before she could react Erimem was on her, raining punches on Ilsa before kicking the back of her knees to sweep Ilsa's legs from beneath her. She pulled her dress aside and dropped a knee to where Ilsa's neck should be.

'These dresses are not suitable for combat,' Erimem complained.

'You're doing fine, love,' Andy said encouragingly and treated herself to a hard kick at Ilsa's backside.

Adam, meanwhile, was struggling with Xandra over the book. Both now had hold of the book and were pulling at it.

Xandra grasped at her necklace and pulled it hard. The metal broke so that she held the snake by the tail. She swung it hard like a miniature whip. The head hit Adam's hand hard and the metal teeth gouged his skin, but he refused to release his hold on the book.

'Stuff this.' Helena's balled fist flew at Xandra. She saw the blow coming and raised her arm to deflect it from her face to her shoulder, but the impact was enough to throw her off balance and Adam won their tug-of-war, ripping the book from her grasp.

They had their prize.

'Run!' Erimem shouted.

All four ran for the exit, passing a dozen startled patrons who had certainly never seen that kind of trouble in *Les Ambassadeurs* before. As soon as they were outside they sprinted for the nearest side street and a moment later, a crackling ball of electricity swept them back to their own time.

When Xandra and Ilsa emerged from the club there was no sign of their prey.

Back in Erimem's villa, the party of four were exhilarated by their success. Feeling pleased with themselves, they quickly made their way to the unlikely hospital ward behind one of Erimem's walls. They quickly worked out which room was Mason's when a nurse ran out.

'I shall call Matron,' was all they heard her say before she disappeared.

'I'll get bromide put in his medication,' Helena promised.

Mason was sitting up in bed, looking pale but considerably improved. He looked at them hopefully. 'I didn't expect to see you again. Staff here won't even tell me which hospital this is.' He sighed. 'It's been days.'

Adam frowned. 'Days?'

Andy nudged him and shook her head. 'We'll explain later, okay?'

'We've got the book,' Adam said, plucking the notebook from his pocket and handing it to Mason.

The agent looked relieved and started flipping through the cause of all their trouble.

And then his frown returned.

'You got the book,' he said, 'but not all the pages.'

'What?' Erimem demanded.

Mason pulled the book open. There were torn edges close to the binding showing where three or four pages had once been.

'Pages have been torn out,' Adam groaned.

Mason nodded. He looked desperately worried. 'Those are the pages with info on the *Resolution*.'

Erimem frowned. 'Resolution to what?'

'The submarine *Resolution*,' Mason explained.

Helena nodded in recognition at the name. 'Britain's first submarine armed with Polaris nuclear missiles,' she said. 'I read about it. I think it's commissioned this year.'

'It's been undergoing sea trials,' Mason said.

There was clearly more to tell. 'And?' Erimem pressed.

Mason looked considerably paler than he had when they arrived. 'And it's due to onboard its stock of nuclear missiles tonight or tomorrow.'

It was obvious why Xandra had taken those particular pages. 'That's what they really want,' Andy said, 'the nukes.'

'Or the missiles and the submarine,' Erimem suggested.

Andy shook her head at the idea. 'They couldn't steal a Royal Navy submarine.' She looked around but nobody could reassure her. 'Could they?'

CHAPTER EIGHT

There are few duties in the armed forces as arduous as serving aboard a submarine. The strains of being underwater for days or even weeks on end, breathing recycled air and facing the thought that even the slightest hint of damage could cause the boat to be crushed in a fraction of a second make submariners a very special breed of sailor.

It also means that several of these Matelots are often found in local pubs and bars around the docks when they are in port, making the most of dry land's freedom, booze and hopefully women while they can.

Dennis Morrison had just been enjoying all of those benefits of being ashore, drinking in the *Pheasant Plucker's Ruin*, which was his favourite pub, with Cathy Norman, who was his favourite girl. In fact, she was his only girl. They'd had some drinks and then gone back to her flat for some fun and games before he had reluctantly set off to return to base. The boat was due to sail in the morning and Dennis was sailing with her. The ship ran two crews and he was going to be on the down crew when they left port, so he wasn't too worried about having a few drinks. Which was for the best, because with all that ale in him, Dennis would not have been a very able seaman.

Unfortunately for Dennis, it also meant that he didn't see the two men following him as he staggered along the quiet road. He was wondering if he might treat himself and finish off the evening like a toff by getting a taxi back to the boat when they moved to within ten yards of him.

A light flared behind Dennis and he recognised it as the headlights of a vehicle coming up behind him. Was he in luck? Was it a taxi?

Dennis turned just in time to see the two men throw themselves at him. He was in no condition to defend himself or to fight them off, and was helpless as the vehicle whose lights he had spotted pulled up alongside them. The back doors of the familiar pug-nosed Bedford van swung open and the struggling Dennis was heaved inside. The doors slammed shut and the van pulled away.

In the streets surrounding the harbour, dozens of sailors were winding their way back to base.

Very few of them were to make it.

However, when the *HMS Resolution* pulled out of port, it was reported that she had a full complement of men and officers on board.

Despite the official records saying the contrary, Able Seaman Dennis Morrison was not among them. Like many of his comrades, Dennis lay naked, still and unmoving in a barn twenty miles from port.

An hour after the *Resolution* left port and eased into the English Channel the members of the crew supposedly on their down time made their way individually to one of the boat's storage compartments where they were issued with firearms by a cadaverously thin man who looked ill-at-ease in a Petty Officer's uniform. Also present was a beautiful dark-haired woman in her mid-thirties, who would have been recognised by any of the patrons of *Les Ambassadeurs* who had spent an hour explaining the previous night's disturbance to the police, as Principessa Xandra Caprice. Genuine submariners would have been appalled to have a woman onboard. They all knew that superstition said that was bad luck. These men had no such concerns.

The counterfeit crew swept through the *Resolution*. They shot down every member of the active crew they met, though their weapons gave a soft airy sound as they fired, rather than the usual harsh bark of gunfire. These weapons had been designed and built to be used in locations like this, where there could be no risk of damage to the surrounding structure or any of the equipment. The guns fired anaesthetic darts containing a fast-acting drug which rendered their target unconscious within five seconds. A deadly toxin could have been used by Xandra Caprice knew that it might be useful to keep the crew alive should their expertise be required. The *Resolution* was a new boat and while she had ordered the plans stolen more than a year before so that they could be sold to Britain's enemies, she was aware that her pirate crew might not fully understand these systems.

It only took nine minutes for the submarine to come under Xandra's command. The Control Room was the last to fall but the active crew were unarmed and could offer no resistance.

Eventually only the officers were left standing.

Captain Arthur Godfrey stared in amazement as Xandra strode into the Control Room. She wore a perfectly cut knee-length black leather dress with high heeled boots that reached over her knees. Around her shoulders she wore some kind of leopard skin stole. She looked at the unconscious bodies strewn around the control room with amusement.

'What a lovely submarine,' she smirked. 'I'll take it.' She gave a theatrical laugh and corrected herself. 'My mistake. I have *already* taken it.' She looked at the officers. 'Who is in command here?'

Captain Godfrey took a step forward. 'I am.'

Xandra raised a pistol and aimed it at Godfrey's face. 'Would you try that again?'

Godfrey swallowed nervously but kept his voice even and calm. 'I'd say you're in charge.'

Xandra Caprice snorted a very superior laugh. 'That's much better, little captain.'

Her dismissal irked Godfrey, and he added, 'For now.'

The arrogant smile was frozen on Xandra's face. 'And then you spoil it,' she said sourly and turned away to inspect the nearest station in the control room. 'Someone hit him, please.'

Godfrey didn't have time to react before a heavy fist clubbed into the side of his face. He dropped to one knee with blood seeping from a cut on his cheek.

'Thank you,' Xandra said, turning her attention back to Godfrey. 'Next time, I will have him kill one of your men. Is that understood?'

'Yes,' Godfrey said. Anyone in their right mind could see that this woman would give the order to kill and enjoy doing it.

'Good,' Xandra said. 'Now, you have orders to follow a set course. She waved a hand to stop Godfrey from speaking. 'You don't have to answer that. I already know it's true. Now I have some new co-ordinates for you.'

John Mason's holographic surgeon had insisted that his patient needed at least another week in hospital and had threatened to set security on Helena and her friends for trying to take the agent from the ward's care. In the end, after giving Mason a sedative, Helena had simply switched the programme off. She had taken a good deal of pleasure from seeing the look of surprise and anger on Grizzler Robertson's face just before he faded away.

Andy had found Mason's home address in 1967 and they had travelled directly into his flat, which sat on the first floor in a quiet Chelsea mews.

The flat was rather Spartan, giving the impression of just being a place where Mason slept rather a home in which he lived.

Nevertheless, Mason had been both surprised and pleased to wake up in his own bed. Nobody missed that his first reaction had been to look at the other side of the bed. He was clearly used to waking up with someone's head on the other pillow, though it may be someone whose name and face he would not bother to remember.

Helena had switched into doctor mode and had explained Mason's condition to him and impressed on him that he still had to relax and avoid any exertion. A rather blunt double entendre from Mason had pressed Helena to suggest the agent might also like to avoid a punch in the mouth. Mason took the hint.

Fifteen minutes after waking they had moved Mason through to his sitting room where he had immediately picked up a red telephone, which he explained was a direct line to the head of his department. The black telephone beside it was a simple regular phone line.

Mason's superior answered on the second ring. After swapping various code words to ensure security, Erimem and her friends sat listening to Mason's half of the conversation.

The first few minutes consisted largely of Mason listening to his chief before he began answering questions.

'I have the book. Not me. I had help... No, not our outfit but our side. They got me treatment for a stab wound and retrieved the book. Well, most of it... Those pages are gone, sir. Torn out... Italian by the name of Xandra Caprice... Yes, that was them at *Les Ambassadeurs*... I'm sure our memberships are still fine, sir.'

'Principessa,' Erimem reminded Mason. 'She is very proud of her little title.'

Mason relayed that information and added, 'It may make her easier to trace.'

The chief spoke for a long minute and Mason listened.

'I don't know who we can trust, sir,' Mason confessed bluntly. He listened again then shook his head. 'I don't think I'm in any condition to chase her down.' The chief spoke again, and this time Mason nodded. 'I will.' A brief pause and then he said, 'And to you, sir,' and he hung up.

'Well?' Helena asked impatiently.

Mason sighed and winced at the pain when he breathed deeply. 'My C.O. is convinced we might have been infiltrated. He's taking his most reliable men to round up the traitors.'

That appeared to have almost nothing to do with their problem, at least superficially. Andy frowned deeply. 'Sounds like there's a huge, big-ass "but" coming.'

Mason didn't disappoint her. 'But the *Resolution* has already set to sea and she's dropped off the radar. She hasn't reported in at her appointed time and she has submerged in the Channel.'

'So she could be going anywhere?' Adam asked.

Mason shook his head. 'Not exactly. We've got strings of ships at running sonar at both ends of the Channel slowly converging so they should find her.'

That was something... but it wasn't much.

'But there is no sign yet?' Erimem asked.

'And that sub is carrying nukes?' Helena added.

Mason nodded grimly. 'Sixteen of them.'

Adam's voice sounded dry. 'I can't think of anything glib to say.'

'Me neither,' Andy admitted. 'And being smart-ass is my thing.'

Erimem snapped them out of their fug. 'Then we must stop these weapons. Do we have any leads?' she asked.

'None,' Mason answered, 'except a potential sighting of the woman who's been calling herself Ilsa Lund at Heathrow but the hair colour and weight don't match.'

'Those can be altered,' Erimem said.

Mason didn't argue. 'She's travelling under an American passport as Anna Kalman.'

Andy clapped her hands together. 'That's her.'

'How can you be sure?' Mason asked.

Anna Kalman,' Andy explained. 'That's the name of Ingrid Bergman's character in *Indiscreet*.' She looked round the blank faces but saw Helena smirking. 'See? I was paying attention earlier. Doesn't anybody watch films anymore?'

Mason reached for the phone. 'I'll have her picked up.'

'No,' Erimem stopped him. 'If your organisation has been compromised she will be warned.'

Helena agreed. 'We'll do it.'

Mason shook his head. 'Look, you helped but you've no authority as far as I know. At least nothing you're willing to talk about.'

'We are doing it anyway,' Erimem said finally. 'We know what she looks like.'

'And we owe the cow a good, hard slap,' Andy added.

Mason chose not to argue. In the light of his limited options this unlikely group were his best, most reliable chance of success. 'In that case, you are temporarily pressganged to the Service for no pay. You'll get ID and weapons from my assistant. I'll make sure she's waiting for you at Heathrow. Trust her, nobody else.'

Adam nodded. 'Understood.'

'We'll need wheels,' Andy said. 'Don't suppose you've got a snazzy motor close by?'

'She already arranged that,' Mason said. 'There's a car waiting outside.'

'All right,' Helena nodded.

Mason reached for the phone and winced in pain. He put his hand to his back. 'And once she's got things set for you I'll ask her if she can get the M.O. up here.' He pulled his hand away from his back. It was slick and red. 'I think I'm bleeding again.'

The foreign agent who had arrived as Ilsa Lund, no sat in the Departure Lounge at Heathrow airport waiting for her flight to be called.

This whole mission had turned into an unmitigated disaster. It was a mess. There were too many people involved, too many different forces trying to get the book, and worst of all, she couldn't identify some of them. Usually she would just kill random elements like that, but the four from the train and the casino had evaded her repeatedly. Until she knew who they were, they were dangerous. She would discover everything about them and then deal with them in her own time. For now, though, her first task was to get out of Britain until things cooled down a bit, and she had to do it quickly just in case Xandra Caprice was insane enough to carry through on her plan.

And she was quite sure Xandra Caprice was insane.

The woman had explained her plan to Ilsa as they escaped from the club and it had terrified her. She knew that she had to be out of Europe as soon as possible. She could deal with whatever needed to be dealt with from the safety of another continent.

She glanced up at the clock, silently urging the time to flow faster.

She eyes stopped.

A familiar and unwelcome figure was moving towards her. The coloured flash in the hair was unmistakeable.

One of the four from the previous night.

And if one was there, the others wouldn't be far behind.

Ilsa rose and began walking towards the busiest part of the Departures Lounge. She could lose herself among the other passengers, and from there find a passenger whose place she could take. The resemblance didn't have to be perfect. Just close enough.

But she had to lose that damn girl with the colour in her hair.

The crowd ahead looked promising. More than enough to lose herself in.

Damn!

There was the man. Tall, short hair, straight back and that disapproving, superior look in his eyes. He had POLICE written all over him.

She turned to cut away from both of her pursuers. The one with curly dark hair was closing on her between two rows of seats.

That could only mean one thing.

Turning, she saw the fourth of the group, the small North African one, striding towards her.

Damn her, she was the most arrogant of the four. She looked like she had always known they would catch up with her.

Ilsa weighed her options. She was surrounded and her chances of escape were almost non-existent. She had enough information to broker a deal with Britain's intelligence services that would mean she never had to serve any time in prison. Of course that would probably result in living a miserable life in some small

Canadian town under an alias to avoid retribution from the people she would have to betray.

But all of that would rely on her surviving the next twenty-four hours.

It would rely on *Europe* surviving the next twenty-four hours.

She looked at the four enemies approaching her.

The man's jacket opened slightly as he moved.

He was wearing a shoulder holster. Even from just the butt of the pistol she recognised it as British Intelligence issue.

So that was who they were. She hadn't been sure but now she knew they were colleagues of Mason. In that case she had no option other than to cut a deal with them.

But she also knew that she couldn't simply surrender to them. There was a good chance that her paymasters or Xandra Caprice were having her watched. If she simply gave in and walked away with these agents it would paint a bigger target on her back.

She would have to be caught rather than surrender... she just wouldn't make it all that difficult for them to catch her.

And there was something about the small dark-skinned woman she just didn't like at all. Something in the disdainful way she looked at Ilsa. In the long, dull years she would have to endure living a quiet life under an alias in a miserable out-of-reach location, she would relish the memory of wiping that superior look from the girl's face.

That was why good sense abandoned Ilsa Lund and she flew at Erimem.

Erimem saw the attack coming and didn't think. She simply reacted as her friend and mentor Antranak had taught her so long ago. She stepped aside at the last possible moment and allowed Ilsa's momentum to take her off balance. She lashed out one foot at the back of Ilsa's knee and the woman stumbled then went down hard. She was back to her feet quickly but not quickly enough. Erimem was already on her, slapping her hands hard over Ilsa's ears. The impact shook Ilsa' equilibrium and gave Erimem the chance to strike hard at her opponent's face and neck. She was aware that her friends had closed off any escape for Ilsa but they held back from joining the fight and kept the crowd, who had gone from startled to curious, at bay.

To her credit, Ilsa regained her composure quickly and adopted a fighting stance Erimem didn't recognise.

Ilsa's attack also came in a style Erimem wasn't familiar with. The blows came in combinations and from angles she didn't expect but Antranak had taught her to observe and to adapt. She covered up and blocked the attack as best she could until she saw a pattern, a rhythm in the style of fighting.

That gave her a chance.

Erimem blocked the left hand thrown by Ilsa and dipped her knees, knowing that the right hand was already coming. The blow sailed over her head and Erimem saw Ilsa was reaching forward, off-balance because of the missed punch. She thrust upwards with her knees, driving her shoulder into Ilsa's midriff and sending Ilsa over her shoulder to land hard on her back.

Ilsa staggered back to her feet but this time she was winded and fighting on the back foot. The crowd had pulled into a circle around them, eager to see the excitement.

Erimem pressed the attack.

Two hard blows to Ilsa's face dipped her knees momentarily and a kick to the stomach sent her backwards until she had her back to a barrier. A twenty-foot drop was behind her and she was surrounded by a crowd, some of whom were obviously armed intelligence agents.

Ilsa raised her hands. 'All right,' she gasped out. 'I give in. I surrender.'

Erimem didn't relax but there was a rumble of disappointment from the crowd that the fight was over.

'You will come with us,' Erimem growled.

Ilsa shrugged. 'All right. I...'

Her voice stopped in a choke. Her eyes widened in surprise and blood began to bubble at the corner of her mouth.

Erimem automatically caught Ilsa as she toppled forwards. Her friends had also quickly joined them.

'She's been shot,' Helena said. 'Twice in the back.' It only took a few moments for the examination to give a result. Helena shook her head silently.

Erimem made no attempt to offer comfort to Ilsa. 'Where is the submarine?' she asked the dying woman. 'They have killed you to stop you from talking. Before you die, you can defeat them. Tell us where the submarine is.'

The life was already going out of Ilsa's eyes but she tried to speak. She coughed, sending a spray of foamy blood over Erimem. She tried again and Erimem leaned closer.

'The road to ruin.'

Ilsa tried to speak again but the life left her, and she slumped.

'The road to ruin,' Erimem repeated.

Helena helped Erimem lower Ilsa to the floor. 'Well, she got one final F-U in before she died.'

Erimem had no more interest in the dead body at her feet. She was looking for the killer. 'Can you see where the gunshots came from?'

Adam was also scanning the area. The terrified, scattering crowd made it almost impossible to see anything. 'No,' he said, 'but it must have been local. No sound of breaking glass and we didn't hear anything so there must have been a silencer.'

'So probably a pistol?' Helena suggested.

'Easier to hide,' Adam agreed. They all moved away from the barrier, still looking for some sign of the shooter.

A distraught holidaymaker in an unfortunate pink and yellow dress pointed at Ilsa in dismay. 'Aren't you going to help her?'

'She is dead,' Erimem said emotionlessly. 'The undertaker can deal with her.'

Andy shrugged and waved for two uniformed policemen to come closer then indicated Ilsa's corpse. 'You two. Take care of that.'

'Yes, ma'am.'

Andy barely had time to smirk at being called "ma'am" before she realised that Erimem was already on her way out of Departures with the others close at her heels.

She ran after her friends.

They hurried through the airport, heading back to where their car was parked. Passengers stared in surprise at Erimem and Helena's blood-soaked clothes. An elderly couple glanced over from staring at a huge map of Europe covering a wall and saw the scarlet stained clothing. An instant later, the old man was shuffling his way towards the door as fast as his ancient feet would carry him, with his wife shouting at him to come back.

'We should report this in to Mason,' Helena said.

'Report what?' Erimem asked. She sounded angry. 'Our complete failure?' She shook her head. 'The Road to Ruin. That means nothing.'

'Wait,' Andy said. She had spotted the old couple's fear and might have been amused by it in other circumstances but there was something about the map they had been staring at.

'What?' Helena asked. 'What is it?'

Andy ignored the question. She was looking at the map, at the English Channel, at the contours of the land on either side of it… 'The channel's closed off, right? Ships with sonar at either end.'

'Yes,' Adam agreed.

Andy pressed on. 'So there's no way for it to hide for long with those navies searching for it.'

'You'd hope so,' Helena nodded.

'So what if it's not in the Channel?' Andy asked simply.

Three blank expressions looked back for an instant then they all understood.

'It's dipped in somewhere?' Adam said.

Andy nodded. 'Yeah.'

Helena examined the map carefully. 'There are a lot of coves and inlets.'

'And rivers,' Adam added.

'Yeah,' Andy said slowly, extending a finger. 'But only one leads here.' She pointed at a location on the map, inland in France. A city sitting on a large, recognisable river.

'The Seine?' Adam asked.

Andy's finger pointed again at a city marked on the Seine. 'It's the submarine's road to *Rouen.*'

'Rouen, not Ruin,' Mason's voice crackled on the phone line. 'Was she giving you a clue or having a last laugh at our expense?'

Erimem and her party were gathered in one of the airport managers' offices around the most modern speakerphone 1967 had to offer, while the manager lurked in the background, irate at having his office commandeered and earwigged desperately to hear what was going on. 'Does it matter?' Erimem asked.

'Not really,' Mason replied. 'Twenty minutes ago this message was received by the UN. Its contents are not public and must remain so.'

Helena looked at the airport's manager. 'You. Out.'

'This is my office,' the manager protested.

Andy drew the pistol she had been issued by MI6. 'And this is a gun. Out!'

The manager ran from the room, slamming the door behind him.

'You got a career as a bouncer, girl,' Helena chuckled as Andy put her pistol back in its shoulder holster.

'We are alone now,' Erimem told Mason. 'Go ahead.'

There was a click and a slightly distorted voice spoke. It was obviously a recording. The voice sounded like Vincente, Xandra's cadaverous right hand thug.

'*Governments of Europe. By now many of you will know that the newest British nuclear submarine has been obtained by our organisation. The boat carries sixteen nuclear missiles. Unless each of the governments pays the amount specified through a Swiss bank by noon tomorrow, each nuclear missile will be launched at a different European city. Not all will be capitals. Every nation must comply and the total must be ten billion pounds. Should even one country fail to do its part, every missile will be launched, even against those who have paid. Any failure will result in the death of millions and the humiliation of every nation in Europe. You must all co-operate and, I believe the phrase is, keep each other honest. The deadline is noon tomorrow, London-time. There will be no negotiation or extension. Details of the Swiss bank and each nation's contributions are attached.'*

There was a click as the message ended.

'That's lunacy,' Helena said.

Adam nodded. 'And that's right up Xandra Caprice's alley.'

'Will the governments pay the money?' Erimem aimed her question at the speakerphone.

'I don't know but I don't see that they have an option,' Mason replied.

Adam puffed his cheeks out. 'And even if they launch the missiles from there nobody will retaliate because... they're in the heart of France.'

Helena rubbed at her chin. 'It's good thinking but how do we know for sure?'

'We don't,' Erimem admitted, 'but it is the best theory we've got.'

They had clearly persuaded Mason enough to take the idea higher. 'I have to inform my superiors and the other governments.'

'Will they believe us?' Erimem asked.

Adam shrugged. 'If someone reports seeing a submarine going up the Seine they'll be all over it.'

'Okay, who does a dodgy French accent?' Andy asked.

'I have French friends,' Mason said.

'I bet you do,' Andy said. Somehow, she made it sound tacky.

Mason didn't rise to the bait. He was all business. 'But the important thing is to get you over there.'

'Us?' Helena asked.

'I'm not sure who you are but you saved my life and got the book back,' Mason's voice crackled back. 'It's not saying much but you're still the people I trust most in this thing.'

Andy humphed. 'You so totally need more friends.'

'How will we get there?' Erimem asked.

Mason answered immediately. 'I'll divert one of a pair of Royal Navy Pumas to pick you up. They've got the SBS on board for the assault on the sub.'

'We're attacking a submarine?' Andy's eyes widened.

'Any of you got scuba experience?' Mason asked.

'Only from a holiday in Greece,' Adam answered.

'Learn quickly,' Mason said. 'Follow instructions till you're onboard and then make sure those missiles don't launch.'

'Is that all?' Andy muttered. 'Have we got time to stop off for something to eat?'

'Eat when you get to France,' Mason answered quickly. 'Oh, one more thing when you get there.'

'Why is this not a surprise?' Helena asked sourly.

Mason ignored her tone. 'The French government hasn't cleared this operation yet. They probably will in time, but just don't be surprised if our allies start shooting at you.'

'One day...' Andy sighed, 'just one day... I'd like to go somewhere that people aren't trying to kill us.'

'That's not today, sorry,' Mason said, without the slightest hint of a genuine apology.

'Is there anything else?' Erimem asked.

'Don't fail or half of Europe dies,' Mason said simply.

'No pressure then,' Helena said sourly.

Adam headed for the door. 'I'll get the greetin'-faced bauchle.' Andy looked to Erimem for a translation, but she shrugged, unable to help. Adam pulled the door open and beckoned for the manager to come back into the room. 'You. Back in here.'

'Are you finished?' the manager asked, sounding ready to go into a full-on strop.

Erimem cut him short. 'A navy helicopter is coming to pick us up,' she barked as if she was giving an order to one of her troops before battle. 'It needs a place to land. Make sure it is close by. We are in a hurry.'

The manager, whose desk seemed to suggest that he didn't manage any important or interesting aspect of the airport, blanched and had the look of a man who wished he had stayed in bed that morning.

The Puma helicopter was initially designed and built by the French company *Sud Aviation Aerospatiale*. Its early tests in 1965 had so impressed a number of other nations that their governments had immediately either ordered the aircraft from the French manufacturer or had arranged for a company in their own country to enter into partnership with the French to build the choppers locally.

In the UK, Westland had been chosen as the partner firm.

Officially, none of their helicopters, designated the Puma HC Mk 1, were due to enter service until 1968, but both the SAS and SBS had obtained early access to the craft to carry out manoeuvres and acquaint themselves with the helicopters.

Initially designed as an all-weather utility craft, the Puma was capable of carrying two tonnes of freight or of ferrying a dozen fully armed troops into battle locations. Though not heavily armed, the helicopter's pair of 1,8000shp Turbomeca Makila 1A1 turboshaft engines gave it a very creditable top speed of around 167 knots, which would get the helicopters the 160 miles from Heathrow to Rouen in just over an hour.

The helicopters had landed so close to the terminal buildings that Erimem and her party only had to run a hundred metres to reach them. Various airport workers looked startled or outraged by these unexpected guests but stopped complaining when heavily armed soldiers in full combat gear including balaclavas dropped to the tarmac.

Erimem's party were met by Major Collins, the officer commanding the troops. Like the other soldiers, the majority of his face was hidden behind a balaclava. After seeing their identification, he urged them into the nearest helicopter.

'Moved some of the lads over to the other chopper so you can travel with me,' Collins said. He appeared to take a moment to weigh them up and work out if there was a leader before looking towards Erimem. 'MI6 said you would have intel we would be able to use.'

'Not a great deal,' Erimem admitted. 'Not as much as we would like.'

'But you did get the sub's course,' the Major pressed.

'Yes,' Erimem nodded. 'Andy worked it out.'

'After you beat it out Ilsa Whatever-her-real-name-was,' Andy said.

How they had obtained the intel was of little interest to Collins. He urged them into the helicopter, and they began clambering in. He had to speak louder to be heard. 'That's more than anyone else had. This woman Caprice's plan... will she go through with it?'

'Don't doubt it for a minute,' Helena shouted over the roar of the rotor blade. 'She's a lunatic.'

'I suppose her course is appropriate enough,' Andy shouted, 'she really is *in-Seine*.' She was obviously disappointed that the gag fell flat. 'Suit yourselves.'

'How will we track the submarine in the river?' Erimem asked.

Major Collins waved for the Lynx's side door to be closed and one of his men heaved it shut. 'The French are working on that,' he answered.

Helena looked at his optimistically. 'And they're not going to shoot at us?'

'I can't promise that,' Collins admitted, 'but hopefully the politicians will have sorted it out by the time we get there.'

'And if they haven't?' Helena pressed.

'Then we will have two sets of people trying to kill us,' Erimem said.

Collins' eyes remained emotionless. 'And my permission to fire back at any of them. What are you armed with?'

Erimem showed the Browning pistol she and the others had been issued with. 'Only these.'

'Pop guns,' Collins said dismissively. He nodded to another soldier who was squashed in and observing the debrief. 'Lieutenant, issue some decent weapons to our guests.'

The lieutenant nodded. 'Yes, sir.'

'We are not exactly dressed for battle,' Erimem said.

Collins was prepared for that. 'We've got full kit for you, but you'll have to change on the go.'

'We understand,' Erimem agreed.

'Do we?' Andy snorted. 'I'm guessing this thing doesn't come with changing rooms.'

Helena gave her friend a sympathetic shrug and reached for the kit being passed out by the lieutenant.

The helicopters took off and set their course south towards the Channel. No official flight plans were lodged and orders were given at the airport to forget ever seeing the military craft.

The interior of the Puma might have been roomy if not for eight soldiers, Erimem's party and all of their gear. Space was at a premium and any hint of self-consciousness and dignity had to be set aside as the newcomers changed into their SBS issued gear. The clothes weren't a perfect fit, but they were close enough.

Erimem was particularly pleased by the weapons on offer. As well as a MAC-10 submachine gun (which seemed to be another of the items the SBS had managed to get hold of before its official distribution) she kept the Browning pistol she had been issued with and helped herself to a pair of Heckler & Koch commando style throwing daggers. They were well balanced and fit comfortably in her hand. She had been trained to fight with blades rather than guns and was more comfortable with a dagger than a pistol.

The others had also taken a full complement of weapons and then assumed seats near Major Collins. The officer had been on the radio all the time they had been changing.

'Have you made any progress?' Helena asked.

'The French were sceptical of your idea the sub was going up the Seine,' Collins replied.

Erimem was quick to spot that the officer had given an incomplete answer. 'But?'

'But they accepted it was possible and put eyes on the river,' Collins continued. 'At one of the shallowest sections, a submarine's wake was spotted.'

'So they can keep track of it?' Erimem asked eagerly.

'Not using sonar,' Collins replied quickly. 'That would tell everyone in the sub that they'd been discovered. The French are observing from the air at a distance and giving us first chance to attack.'

'And they're not going to shoot at us?' Andy prodded hopefully.

'They're giving us thirty minutes to take the sub,' Collins said. 'One second over that, or at the first sight of any kind of launch they're hitting the boat with everything they have to sink it.'

Helena added the postscript Collins had left off. 'Whether we're on board or not.'

The major nodded. 'Precisely.'

The lieutenant chose to offer a suggestion and elected to make the worst recommendation possible. 'Perhaps you women should stay behind while we…'

Adam was simply shaking his head. 'Oh, mate. Wrong thing to say.'

'Less of that bollocks,' Andy all but growled.

'We are all experienced in combat,' Erimem said. Just a bit too calmly to be anything but annoyed and not hiding it very well.

Adam tried to explain. 'Any of these three could beat the crap out of me,' he told the lieutenant.

'But we wouldn't,' Helena reassured him.

'Unless we really felt like it,' Andy grinned.

Erimem did not join in the joking. 'How will we get on board the submarine?'

'The French navy are going to help us with that,' Major Collins answered. 'I believe they're commandeering the kit we need just now.'

* * * * *

The *Bernard Huelgoat* was a large, research vessel, initially built for scientific expeditions. It was clearly a civilian vessel and unarmed.

The lack of weapons had concerned Andy as the two Pumas had landed on the research boat's deck.

The soldiers disembarked, lugging their gear and were led away by the lieutenant.

'The equipment we need is over this way,' Major Collins shouted over the sound of the departing helicopters.

Collins led the way to a railing which ran around a huge square well at the centre of the ship. Looking down into the opening, they saw that there were a pair of small submarines which launched into the water from this well in the middle of the ship.

He pointed at the small subs. '*Those* are the kit we need.'

The *Bernard Huelgoat* had already pulled away from its moorings by the time the Royal Navy helicopters landed on it and made its way to the centre of the river, moving slowly along the channel as is it was heading out to sea.

To anyone watching it was a perfectly mundane departure.

What none of those observers saw was that more than a dozen heavily armed military personnel had crammed their way into two small exploration submersibles which had been winched into the water.

The research vessel had made its way to the deepest part of the river. That would be expected of such a large ship.

It would also act as the perfect cover for a submarine moving along the river. Any hint of a wake left in the water would be put down to the propellers of the ship on the surface.

The submarine played its part perfectly and took the bait, easing its way under the research vessel. As the two craft passed, the pair of small submersibles disappeared beneath the surface and made their way after the *Resolution*. One of the submersibles moved towards the *Resolution* to the for'ard and starboard while the other went to port and aft. In unison, both submersibles

152

deployed tubes of a corrugated and durable-looking black material which fastened to the Resolution's hull.

'They'll find the boat harder to handle with us attached,' Major Collins told Erimem, 'but we're in the wash from the research ship up top. They'll put it down to that. It'll scramble things enough for us to lock on undetected.'

Adam looked uncertainly at the little tube connecting the two craft. 'Can I ask where we're locking on?'

'You can ask, but I'm not allowed to give any details on that,' Collins replied. 'Even I don't have the security clearance to know what I know. I may have to arrest myself after this is over.'

Adam appreciated the attempt at a joke but Erimem was focused completely on their mission.

'As long as it gets us aboard, is it important?' she asked.

Collins shook his head. 'No,' answered. 'Be ready to board in one minute. My men will take the lead.'

In unison, both submersibles attained entry to the *Resolution* by breaching emergency escape hatches. The SBS troops poured into the submarine.

The troops entering from the rear swept through the narrow metal rabbit warren. The first sighting of the enemy resulted in a swift, one-sided skirmish in which an SBS trooper silently choked out one of the fake sailors.

Andy and Helena had been assigned to this party while Erimem and Adam were in the assault on the for'ard sections.

Helena picked up the pirate's fallen gun and inspected it. 'Tranquiliser gun,' she said.

The SBS lieutenant took the pistol and looked it over quickly. 'They don't want to cause damage to the ship's systems.'

That was something Andy could certainly believe. 'With sixteen nuclear weapons around do you blame them?'

'They're trying to blow up sixteen cities in Europe,' Helena reminded her. 'I'll blame them for anything.'

A sailor appeared ahead. He had time to look surprised and reach for his pistol before a Heckler & Koch dagger sang through the air and slammed into his chest. He dropped, gasping in surprise. A trooper moved quickly and silenced him permanently.

'Take the next one alive,' the lieutenant ordered. 'We need to know what happened to the real crew.'

Two more sailors appeared ahead, and this time they were quick enough to grab their pistols. The first shot caught Andy on the shoulder.

The impact spun Andy around ad she dropped to the deck. 'Oh, shit.'

The SBS returned fire, cutting down the sailors in seconds but the noise of their machine guns was echoing through the submarine.

'Bang goes the element of surprise,' Helena said.

'Um... Helena...' Andy was looking at her shoulder. A traquiliser dart was embedded in her fatigues.

Andy winced at the sudden realisation that her shoulder ached. 'Oh, bollocks.'

Towards the front of the *Resolution*, Major Collins was leading his men through the submarine's tight interior, making for the Control Room.

One of the soldiers, carrying a boosted radio set, reported to the officer. 'Word from aft, sir. They've engaged the enemy.'

'Do they know we are here?' Collins asked.

Two men sloppily dressed in sailor uniforms and carrying pistols emerged from a doorway. Their eyes widened at the sight of Collins' unit and they opened fire.

'They know about us now,' Adam muttered.

Erimem didn't wait for Collins to order his men to return fire. She was already moving towards the sailors. 'Then we must hurry!' she shouted.

Erimem sprinted along the narrow corridor, firing two warning shots at the enemy sailors. They ducked back into cover. She had already thrown herself feet first along the metal floor by the time they looked out. She grabbed one leg of each and pulled hard, sending both men toppling hard to the floor. One cracked his head on a thick, metal pipe as he fell.

Major Collins and his men quickly disarmed the sailors and restrained them.

Only the eyes of the SBS troops were visible but they all looked at Erimem with surprise and respect for the way she had taken down the two pirates.

'We need to interrogate them,' Adam said. Poking one of the pirates with his boot.

'We have no time to ask questions,' Erimem said briskly. 'Torture would be the most efficient plan.'

Collins' eyes widened in surprise.

'She's not kidding, Major,' Adam said. 'Give her one minute and they'll tell us everything they know.'

Collins didn't flinch from the idea of forcing their captives to talk. 'To save these cities I'd let her torture the Queen.'

Erimem raised one of her daggers towards the nearest of the pirates.

They both started babbling.

'We will tell you anything you want to know.'

'We will tell you everything.'

Adam checked his watch. 'Less than five seconds. That's a new record, even for you.'

'We are in a hurry,' Erimem answered quickly. She eased her dagger closer to the nearest pirate.

Major Collins took that as his cue to speak. 'You two, start talking or start bleeding.'

At the other end of the submarine, the SBS troops were meeting resistance from the fake crew manning the *Resolution*. The SBS was making headway, but it was slower than they had hoped.

Helena had dragged Andy into cover so that she could examine the wound on her friend's shoulder.

'Are you feeling drowsy?' she asked, and then pulled at Andy's collar so that she could see the skin where she had been hit.

Andy thought briefly. 'Not so's you'd notice,' she said.

'You're in luck.' Helena released Andy's collar and fished in her fatigues. A moment later she held up the thin, needle-like point of the tranquiliser dart. 'Your armour stopped took the hit and broke the sharp point off. You'll have bruising across that shoulder but nothing else.'

Andy sighed in relief. 'I am definitely kicking somebody in the balls for this.'

'Just make sure they're not on our side,' Helena said, helping Andy back to her feet.

Two more sailors appeared, but this time they took refuge behind jutting metal outcrops on the walls.

The lieutenant wasted no time in dealing with the new threat. 'Stun grenades.'

Withing seconds a pair of grenades were thrown. They detonated by the two hiding sailors. They screamed and staggered towards the troopers. One was shot in the leg and the other was quickly clubbed down.

'Word from the Major,' A trooper holding a small radio called to the lieutenant. 'Told us where the real crew are being held.'

'That's good work,' Helena said appreciatively.

The lieutenant took the report of the room where the crew was held captive. 'Right. We release the sailors and disable the missiles.'

Andy rubbed at her aching shoulder. 'And the Major's mob take the Control Room.' She sniffed nervously. 'Sounds easy when you say it fast.'

The lieutenant waved his troops forward. 'This way.'

Standing in the Control Room of the *Resolution*, Vincente could tell that things were no longer going to plan. He has seen his lackeys talking animatedly on their radios. One of those flunkies ran to Vincente's side. 'Reports are coming that two forces have made it on to the submarine, sir,' the sailor said nervously, 'coming at us from the front and the back of the boat.'

Vincente didn't bother acknowledging the sailor who delivered the report. He tilted his head back and spoke clearly and loudly. 'Principessa.'

Xandra Caprice's voice came from a small speaker on the wall. 'I heard, Vincente,' she said languidly. 'There is no reason to change our plans.'

'They will not find you?' Vinccente asked worriedly.

Xandra laughed derisively. 'Of course not. They are just stupid policemen.' She sounded confident and reassured. 'Continue with your orders. Begin launch procedures.'

'Yes, Principessa,' Vincente said. 'Hide from them. Stay safe.'

'The world should hide from me.' Xandra Caprice's voice oozed arrogance. 'Now do as I order.'

That was clearly the end of the conversation. Vincente rounded on his crew, barking a stream of orders. 'You heard her. Lock targets and prepare to launch all sixteen missiles.'

The ersatz crew hurried to obey.

A klaxon started wailing and the interior of the submarine was given a darker hue by flashing red lights on the walls.

'What's that?' Adam asked, though in his heart he already knew the answer.

'They've started arming procedure,' Major Collins answered.

'Meaning?' Adam pressed.

Erimem beat Collins to the answer. 'Meaning we have to hurry.'

The SBS attack at the rear of the submarine was dangerously close to stalling.

Andy gave voice to the frustration she could sense building around her. 'We're not moving fast enough.'

Helena agreed and understood the crew's tactics. 'They just need to hold us up till they can launch.'

'Stuff that.' Andy unslung her rifle and quickly went through the checks they had been shown earlier.

'What are you doing?' Helena protested. 'Have you ever used one of those before?'

Andy looked offended by the question. 'I kicked your arse at *Call of Duty* more than once.' She pointed along the corridor, close to where two sailors were taking cover behind a large protruding bulkhead. 'See that sign by the pipe?'

Helena looked quickly and saw a thick pipe running from floor to ceiling. It was marked DANGER HEAT. She instantly knew that Andy was about to do something unbelievably stupid. 'You're not...'

Andy squeezed the trigger and fired a long burst at the pipe. 'Not what?' she shouted. A second burst aimed at exactly the same spot ripped the metal pipe open. A thick cloud of scalding hot steam erupted outwards engulfing the two sailors hiding nearby. They screamed in pain.

'You bloody lunatic.' Helena thumped Andy's arm. 'How did you know that was just steam?'

'Bit of a guess,' Andy admitted.

Helena was ready to continue castigating Andy but the soldiers were already surging forward.

'Move! Now! The lieutenant shouted.

However well-trained Xandra Caprice's people were, they were no match for the SBS, who quickly overran the area and took down the few sailors still trying to defend against them.

Andy and Helena let the SBS subdue the enemy and followed just a few steps behind. Andy stopped a few paces from the ruptured pipe she had shot and sucked her lip as she looked at the steam venting into the passage. 'Just a thought. This won't be radioactive, will it?'

'You ask that *now*?' Helena hustled Andy past the pipe. 'Bit bloody late for that question, isn't it?'

They hurried after the lieutenant and found him at a locked door just as two of his men dragged away a sailor who had been standing sentry at the door.

'Locked door, sir,' one of the troops said.

'Obviously,' the young officer snapped. 'Open it.'

Two of the SBS troops kicked the door in unison. On the third kick it opened. The frightened and angry crew looked out of the mess room which had been their prison for hours.

'Are you lot the crew?' Helena asked.

A naval officer looked surprised to see women on his boat but answered quickly. 'Yes. I'm Lieutenant Davis.'

'Right,' Helena said. 'Good. We need your help.'

Davis moved forward to join his rescuers. 'What's been happening? How did you get on board?'

Helena answered the important points of his question. 'We're near Rouen and about to use your missiles to blow up Europe.'

The naval officer winced. 'I heard the alarm. Does she still have the Control Room?'

The SBS lieutenant answered. 'We're moving on it but we haven't taken it yet.'

Davis digested the information. 'Then we have to disable the missiles themselves.'

'How do we do that?' Andy asked.

Davis was already moving along the passage. 'We need to get to the controls down here.'

The crew spilled out. Davis called for a few men to follow him and the others were instructed to arm themselves and follow the orders of their rescuers.

'You know what to do?' the lieutenant asked hopefully.

Davis nodded. 'Of course.'

Helena hurried to keep up with the sailor. 'By the way… *she*?'

Davis nodded again. 'Italian accent, looks a bit like Gina Llolobrigida, vicious as a rattlesnake.'

'Gorgeous Italian loonie with big knockers?' Andy translated.

'That's her,' Davis confirmed. 'With a mouth like that you should be a sailor.'

Helena looked surprised. 'She's on board herself?'

'Humiliated the captain in front of the crew,' Davis said.

Andy grimaced sourly. 'That sounds like her. I'm with you, though - surprised she's on board.'

Helena shrugged. 'If you can work out what's happening in her head… see a shrink.'

The SBS lieutenant barked back at his troops. 'Get those men out and get them armed.'

'Where do we have to go to control the missiles?' Andy asked Davis.

The sailor pointed the way ahead. 'Follow me. I'll show you.'

Progress to the Control Room had been swift and brutal for Major Collins' squad. They had met any opposition with efficient ruthlessness.

It came as no surprise that the entrance to the Control Room was sealed.

Collins and his men had come prepared for this possibility.

Two of the soldiers placed compact charges around the outer edges of the door.

Adam was the only one who was nervous. 'Um, this is a submarine, remember? And we're underwater? I mean, is setting off explosions what you'd call a good idea?'

'We know what we're doing,' Collins said.

'Fuses set,' one of the soldiers called.

Move,' Collins told Adam. 'If you don't, that *would* be a bad idea.'

Erimem grabbed Adam's arm and hauled him back into cover.

Lieutenant Davis, who had been the Resolution's acting Executive Officer, led the small party down one level by a vertical ladder to a control room that to Andy's eyes was both futuristic and retro. There were dials, readings and meters, but in her own time she would have expected all of that information to be on a computer screen.

'This it?' Andy asked Davis.

It's not for boiling the kettle.

Pardon me for asking. Guessing those lights aren't for Christmas either.

Davis swore. 'No. It means the launch procedure has started.'

'So how do we stop it?'

Davis shook his head. 'I don't know.

The four carefully timed explosions ripped the Control Room's doors off in a deafening cacophony of fire, smoke and noise.

SBS troops made the first incursion into the Control Room but Erimem and Adam were close behind them.

Most of the pirates were stunned by the sudden force of the explosion. The few who were still upright and ready to fight were put down very quickly.

Quickly looking around, Erimem saw the skinny figure of Vincente with his hand on a key in a control panel.

'That's got to be the weapons launch controls,' Adam said.

He started to move forward but Erimem was faster. Her arm flashed forward and a Heckler & Koch dagger tumbled through the air. It ripped into Vincente's wrist and yanked it to the side where it was pinned into the metal panel.

Vincente screamed against the pain from the torn flesh and broken bones in his wrist, but he looked at Erimem with triumph. 'You are too late. The launches have begun.'

In the nuclear missiles' control area, Erimem's voice crackled from Andy's radio. 'Andy, you need to stop the missiles.'

'We can't,' Andy answered immediately. 'They've already started to fire up.'

'We know,' Erimem crackled.

Andy watched Lieutenant Davis trying various controls without any success. 'Can't you do anything from up there?' she asked Erimem.

The reply was immediate. 'Nothing.'

Andy's reply was instinctive. 'Oh, shite!'

'How do they launch?' Erimem asked. 'We need more information.

Andy looked to Davis.

He explained as concisely as possible. 'Silo opens, the missile gets released and the rockets ignited.'

'What if the silos didn't open?' Andy asked.

'They couldn't take off,' Davis answered. He thought for a long second. 'The rocket engines might still ignite, mind.'

Andy weighed that up. 'Bad for the sub but Europe doesn't wind up crispy fried?'

'More or less,' Davis agreed.

'Can you stop the silos opening?' Andy pressed.

Davis nodded slowly. 'I think there's a way.'

'Good man,' Andy said. 'It's in your hands.' She spoke to the radio. 'Erimem, I think we have an idea. No guarantees it'll work, though.'

'Try it anyway,' Erimem instructed, 'and good luck.'

'What are you going to do?' Andy asked.

Erimem's reply did not fill Andy with optimism.

'We need to crash the submarine,' Erimem said.

There was a nervous pause before Andy's voice came back through Erimem's radio. 'What did you say?'

'We need to crash the submarine.' Erimem repeated.

Captain Godfrey, the submarine's commander, reacted angrily to the suggestion. 'We've already lost it once. I'm damned if I'll let some girl crash it.'

Major Collins ignored the captain. 'What are you thinking?' he asked Erimem.

She explained. 'If they can not keep the silos closed, what if we rolled this submarine in its belly or on its side?' Her eyes widened. 'Surely the missiles would simply stay in the water?'

Adam wore a similar expression to the concerned sailors assuming positions around them. 'I don't think they're built for rolling like that,' he told Erimem.

She nodded her agreement. 'Which is why I think we should use the research ship.'

Adam was quiet for a second. 'How would it work?'

Captain Godfrey protested again. 'I am in command of this vessel and I will not let you crash it.'

Major Collins took two strides and stood directly in front of Godfrey. 'Listen,' he barked, 'as far as we are concerned, she is in command and our mission is to stop those missiles launching. Get in our way and I'll lock you up myself.'

'You're lucky,' Adam told Godfrey. 'She'd probably just shoot you.'

Godfrey didn't back down from the major. 'I will make a complaint to the ministry.'

Collins shrugged. 'Who do you think sent her?'

'This is madness!' Godfrey erupted.

Adam was not fazed by the sailor's outrage. 'That's what we do apparently.'

Erimem used her hands to mimic the two vessels moving towards each other. 'If we come in from the side…'

Collins nodded. 'We'd need them to be travelling faster than us.'

'Can we communicate that to them?' Erimem asked.

Collins waved one of his men forward. 'We'll get the message out.'

Helena peered over Andy's shoulders as Lieutenant Davis operated a series of buttons.

Davis sounded very worried. 'Did she really say she was going to crash the submarine?'

'I'm sure there's a reason for her going loopy,' Andy answered. 'There usually is.'

'Usually,' Helena reiterated.

Andy grimaced. 'Well… sometimes.'

'There,' Davis blurted triumphantly. 'This is the control we…' his voice tailed off, '…damn.'

Andy did not like the sound of that. 'That's a bad "damn", isn't it?'

'It's already engaged,' Davis said.

'In non-sailor?' Helena urged.

Davis shook his head miserably. 'I can't stop the silos from opening.'

'Can you do *anything* to stop the launch?' Andy asked.

Davis shook his head. 'No.' But his eyes fell on a reading and they could almost hear him brain whirring. 'Wait. I might be able to put an emergency cycle through it. That would give us an extra ninety seconds.'

'Ninety seconds,' Adam repeated the words Andy had reported.

'Is that enough?' Major Collins asked.

Another klaxon wailed and everyone looked to Captain Godfrey.

'They're preparing for launch,' Godfrey said.

Erimem didn't hesitate. 'Crash the boat,' she said.

Godfrey was still searching for another alternative. 'I don't think…'

'Do it or go!' Erimem bellowed at Godfrey.

Collins nodded his agreement. 'You heard her.'

'All right.' Godfrey conceded defeat and issued orders to his crew. 'Take us to starboard and take us up to periscope depth.'

Families out for a walk by the beautiful river Seine were shocked to see the periscope of a submarine appear in the river. That feeling was multiplied several times over when the top of the sub's sail became visible.

The *Resolution* began turning in an arc. Back along the river, the *Bernard Huelgoat* had also turned. The large research ship and the submarine were on a collision course.

There was plenty of time for both craft to change course. The watching public screamed as if their voices might be heard by the sailors.

The two huge boats converged relentlessly until the side of the *Bernard Huelgoat* struck the sail of the submarine with a terrible screech of rending metal.

The research ship's weight and speed pushed the submarine over onto its side and then began to scape over the hull accompanied by the horrified screams of the public.

* *| * * *

There were also screams on board the *Resolution*. It had tilted to almost ninety degrees to starboard. A few sailors clung to their posts but most had been thrown to the wall which now acted as their floor.

Back among the launch controls, the crew and the troops were in disarray. A light flashed red. It didn't take a sailor to understand that.

'We're launching,' Andy breathed.

The hatches over each of the missile silos opened and the river surged in, but the missiles could not launch. As the *Bernard Huelgoat* pushed past the sail, the submarine began to right itself. But the sail now protruded up through the ship's inner well and the rest of the submarine was trapped under the ship. As the launch system tried to eject the missiles, they simply rose a few feet and impacted on the bottom of the ship's hull before dropping back into position.

'Did it work?' Major Collins picked himself up from the metal floor. Most of the personnel in the Control Room had been thrown about quite badly.

'Launch failure!' Andy's voice yelled over the radio. 'Not one left its silo.'

Erimem was still concerned. 'Will they explode inside the submarine?'

'No,' Captain Godfrey said. 'They hadn't fully armed. They're safe'

Erimem finally let herself breathe a heavy sigh and then allowed her shoulders to sink. 'That is definitely a relief.'

'So we're done?' Adam asked hopefully.

Erimem shook her head. They still had one part of their mission to complete. 'No.' She turned and looked at Xandra

Caprice's skeletal minion, Vincente. He was still pinned to the panel with her dagger through his wrist.

'Oh, him,' Adam sad sourly. 'Man, that looks like it hurts.'

Erimem looked at the blood dripping down the panel's metal surface. 'You should let a physician see that.'

On cue, Andy and Helena ran into the Control Room, looking thoroughly pleased with themselves.

'And here's one now,' Adam said.

Helena beamed at his friends. 'Don't know how the crashing thing worked but... brilliant.'

'Only worked because of Andy's extra ninety seconds though,' Adam pointed out.

'Team effort,' Andy said modestly, but she happily soaked up the praise.

Erimem brought them back down to earth. 'But we must still find the Caprice woman.'

Vincente sneered at her. 'You will never find her.'

'Where is she?' Erimem demanded. 'We can scour the ship for her.'

'Go ahead,' Vincente answered defiantly.

Erimem read the situation quickly. 'She is not on the submarine. She was put ashore somewhere along the river.'

Despite his suffering, Vincente laughed. 'And she is already somewhere safe.'

'Damn,' Andy cursed. 'I really wanted to see her in jail.'

'As did I,' Erimem agreed.

Helena turned to Collins. 'Major, you better get hold of London. We need to tell them about the one that got away.'

CHAPTER NINE

The SBS, along with Erimem's party had flown back to England in their Lynx helicopters, leaving the *Resolution* and *Bernard Huelgoat* to be retrieved and returned to their respective ports for repair.

Xandra Caprice's lackeys, in particular Vincente, would be flying back to England soon after to undergo extreme interrogation.

John Mason met with Erimem's party in an office near Regent's Park. It carried the nondescript name of an import business on the front plaque but the building played home to an integral part of Britain's secret services.

Mason sat uncomfortably behind a large wooden desk with his guests on stiff old chairs in front of him. 'Sorry it's only me,' he said. 'My chief has rounded up a number of traitors, all linked to the politician at the heart of all of this, and is giving them absolute hell. He's tied up with the PM. I believe there are a few other cabinet ministers in trouble, too.'

'Same as always, then,' Andy said. 'Nothing changes there.'

'Quite,' Mason agreed and then quickly moved on. 'Well, the *Resolution* should be all right. The acting captain isn't your biggest admirer, but you all managed to avoid Europe being blown up, and that's the main thing.' He gave a tight smile. 'Plus, the French didn't shoot at you.'

'Brucie Bonus,' Andy agreed.

Mason's eyebrow rose quizzically. 'A who what?'

Andy waved the question away. 'Never mind.'

Erimem was not happy that they had not completely fulfilled their mission. 'It is a shame that we did not catch Xandra Caprice.'

'Yes,' Mason agreed, 'I'd have liked to put her in a cage, but all is not lost there.'

Erimem leaned forward keenly. 'You know where she is?'

'We've got an idea,' Mason answered cagily. 'Hours before you attacked the sub, a helicopter flew without permission from just back along the river. It kept low but it was picked up a few times.'

'Do you know where it went?' Erimem pressed impatiently.

'The Alps,' Mason answered. 'It was last seen about ten miles from a mountain retreat, a schloss that used to belong to the Compte de Traberre.'

'Who does it belong to now?' Adam asked.

'A trading company,' Mason replied. 'A trading company based in Naples, Italy.'

The Italian connection was unlikely to simply be a coincidence and they all knew it.

'That is where she is,' Erimem said certainly.

'I think so,' Mason confirmed.

Andy sighed. 'So, I assume we're going to get her?'

The attack came at dawn.

Six of the British Army's Westland Scout helicopters in the white livery of the covert Arctic Deployment Unit, took off from a French military base near Lyon long before the sun rose and refuelled once before beginning their approach to the target property where Principessa Xandra Caprice was believed to have taken refuge.

The helicopters kept low and crossed undetected, and without permission, into Swiss airspace. They followed the contours of the mountains, avoiding towns and villages on the Alpine slopes. The engines protested at the additional strain put on them by the cold air thinning as they gained altitude. The approach was timed to coincide with the sun rising over the surrounding snow covered peaks. The slopes beneath the helicopters had long since turned white as they flew towards the permanently frozen summits.

Seated on a four-seat bench in the back of the third Scout in formation, Erimem, Andy, Helena and Adam huddled together. The small heater at the front of the helicopter was proving to be inadequate to the task of keeping the small helicopter above freezing.

'I'll be glad to get outside,' Andy complained. 'At least when we're moving we can stay warm.'

'Stop complaining,' Helena scolded mildly. 'You said you missed snow at Christmas.'

Andy glowered back. 'Is this Christmas? You hear Noddy Holder?'

The pilot's voice crackled in their headsets. 'The schloss is in view. Sixty seconds.'

Another voice crackled in their ears repeating 'Sixty seconds.'

Erimem took a deep breath and inspected her rifle. It was the same model she had taken onto the submarine with the SBS. 'Is everyone prepared?' she asked.

Replies with varying amounts of enthusiasm came back.

'Nowhere I'd rather be. Well, apart from the Maldives.'

'If I have to be.'

'Can we just get this over with?'

Erimem smiled to herself. The answers were more or less as she had anticipated. She tensed the muscles in her neck and then relaxed, taking a deep breath. She took another deep breath and closed her eyes to focus herself.

When she opened her eyes she was standing by the harbour an ancient Alexandria. She recognised her grandfather's favourite spot immediately. Sure enough he was sitting looking out over the water, observing the fishing boats making their way back to land.

To her surprise she felt Adam's hand on her arm. 'I don't want to ask the obvious,' he said, 'but what the actual eff?'

She squeezed his hand reassuringly. 'I'm sure I will be able to explain it all, I promise.' She humphed. 'As soon as this old rogue explains it to me.'

The old Pharaoh waved them forward impatiently. 'Hurry up, hurry up. It's about to start.'

Erimem led the few steps to her grandfather's side. 'Why are we here?'

The old man took a deep breath of the sea air and smiled to himself. 'This was never your task to perform, child,' he said. 'This task was to see if your friends could be trusted.'

'You have sent Andy and Helena alone?' Erimem bristled at the thought of her friends going into danger without her.

Her grandfather was not bothered one bit. 'Yes.'

'So why am I not there?' Adam asked.

The old man scratched at the end of his nose and peered at the young policeman. 'Because you've been sharing a bed with my grand-daughter and I need more time to weigh you up.'

'Grandfather!' Erimem was genuinely flustered. 'My love life is not a matter for discussion. Not with you, anyway.'

Her grandfather laughed off her concern. 'Talking about sex is as close as I get to it these days.' He peered intently at Adam. 'You're very pale. Didn't notice that last time.'

'I'm Scottish,' Adam answered quickly. 'We're either pale blue or burning lobster red. No middle ground between them. Nothing we can do about that. It's science.'

His answer made the old pharaoh laugh.

'Can we turn our attention back to Andy and Helena, please?' Erimem asked pointedly.

'Oh, of course,' the old man nodded. 'Shall we see what they're up to?'

'Can we help them?' Erimem asked.

'No, no, no.' Her grandfather was appalled by the idea. 'Where would the fun be in that? No, this is about *them*.'

The tranquil surroundings of the harbour faded and darkened. In the blink of an eye they were sitting in a darkened cinema. There were alone, in comfortable reclining seats, and the old man was playing gooseberry by sitting between Erimem and Adam.

The projector flickered into life sending a sweeping panning shot of azure blue skies and the crisp white peaks of Alpins mountains. Six British Army Westland Scout helicopters flew in tight formation towards a magnificent schloss which looked like it dated back at least two hundred years or more with rather gothic architecture. Figures could be seen running on the terraces, panicking at the sight of these incoming aircraft.

The picture cut quickly to the inside of one of the helicopters where Andy and Helena were looking around in alarm.

'Where the hell are Erimem and Adam?' Helena demanded, looking around the small cabin.

Andy fumed. 'If they've nipped home for a bit of hello-folks-and-what-about-the workers I will be so pissed off.'

Helena shook her head. 'They'd never do that.'

'That's true,' Andy conceded. 'She'd never miss out on a good punch-up.'

The schloss was close and they could hear gunfire from below. 'We'll have to worry about that later.'

'I bet you it's her bloody grandad,' Andy seethed. 'I could boot him right in the bollocks. And I need to stop threatening to do that to people.'

The Pharaoh cackled his approval, sucked at his drink through a straw, bit into a choc-ice and then reached into Erimem's box of popcorn. Erimem began to complain – about not being with her friends in battle rather than that her popcorn was being pilfered – but the old man waved a hand to quiet her.

'Now, shush. Let's watch the film and see what happens.'

Had anyone else dared talk to her that way there was a fair chance Erimem would have snapped their hand off at the wrist and force-fed it to them. Instead, she settled for glaring at her grandfather for a moment before picking up the tub of ice cream that had appeared in her seat's cup holder. There were three scoops inside – strawberry, chocolate and one she didn't recognise but which was utterly delicious.

She turned her eyes back to the screen and watched Andy and Helena drop the two metres from the helicopter to the terrace below.

Andy did as she had been told and bent her knees as she landed. She dropped to the ground, rolled and was back up on her feet in what she thought was one swift movement.

Somehow Helena managed to have landed later and got up earlier.

They had landed on the largest of the three main terraces. This was the main outdoor socialising area, while the one at the top had tables for eating outdoors and the lower seemed to have marking for some kind of curling-like game.

All three terraces were now battle zones.

The men defending the schloss were well trained and armed but the army troops were better and more numerous. The battle was quickly becoming one sided and Xandra Caprice's mercenaries fell in quick succession, it was in danger of becoming a rout.

'This is all a bit one-sided,' Andy said.

'Too one-sided,' Helena agreed. She ducked and grabbed Andy's arm, dragging her down behind a heavy planter. A chunk of its corner exploded into dust as bullets slammed into it.

Helena looked out and saw one of Xandra's mercenaries trying to reload his machine gun. She moved quickly, running straight at him and smashing the butt of her rifle into his jaw. He staggered, dazed. She and Andy each grabbed one of the man's arms and hurled him over the restraining wall overlooking the slopes. His scream lasted longer than they had expected before he landed in a deep drift.

They turned to go back towards the schloss and had to move aside as a soldier hurled a mercenary in the same direction as their own victim.

That encouraged Andy and Helena to move, sprinting towards the full-length glass doors leading into the schloss. Helena shattered the doors with a blast from her rifle and they ran inside.

They had come in to a large lounge area filled with sofas and a huge dining table. A door led out into a corridor with doors leading off it. The only people in any of them were a pair of terrified chefs who made a half-hearted attempt to brandish kitchen knives but backed off when Helena aimed her rifle at them.

'Stairs,' Andy shouted from behind her. She was at the top of an elegant, beautifully decorated stairwell.

Helena ran to join her. 'Who'd run away?'

Looking down they saw a familiar head of thick dark hair and then Xandra Caprice looked up and laughed. '

There she is!' Helena said.

Andy raised her rifle and fired but she was too late. Xandra had already moved off the stairs. 'Damn. Missed her.'

'Forced her off the stairs, though,' Helena said. 'She must have gone into a room down there.'

They began making their way carefully down the stairs, weapons raised and ready to fire. At the level Xandra had been at, there was only one door. They prepared to go through.

'Be careful,' Helena said. 'She's mad but not stupid.'

Andy looked around the stairwell and smiled. 'We're not so daft, either.'

Andy and Helena entered Xandra Caprice's office quickly and efficiently. They could easily have passed for trained agents.

Unfortunately, Xandra Caprice was waiting for them. She was standing behind a desk that must have come from one of the most fashionable boutique shops in London or Paris. It was curved and moulded of some sort of gleaming white plastic. It seemed out of place with the extraordinary array of classical art around the room… everything from early prints of novels to unknown pieces of art by the great painters and statues which had been stolen from those who had earlier stolen them from their rightful owners.

Xandra had a muscular bodyguard on either side of her. All three had guns aimed at Andy and Helena.

Helena's lips pursed. 'Three against two is hardly fair.'

Xandra didn't move her gaze from them. 'Coming into my house without asking is hardly polite.'

'Pot and kettle given that you went onto a submarine without the captain's permission,' Andy answered.

Xandra feigned a coy expression. 'That was very naughty of me.'

'You're a very naughty girl,' Andy said. 'Normally I'd say that's a good thing and right up my alley, but in your case I make an exception.'

Andy and Helena began circling the office, apparently looking for a better position, but Xandra and her bodyguards kept their weapons trained on the intruders, who were now standing with their backs to another full length window looking out over the pristine white slope.

'Aren't there usually four of you?' Xandra asked.

Helena answered apologetically. 'Not sure what happened to the other two. Looks like they decided to sit this one out.'

'What a pity,' Xandra said sadly. 'Still, killing two of you will be satisfying enough.'

'Something to keep you happy while you rot in jail,' Helena said.

'Without parole,' Andy added. 'Or make-up.'

That simply made Xandra Caprice laugh outrageously. 'Oh, darling, you're so innocent. I'm not going to jail. I'm *rich*, you silly girl.'

Andy let the patronising insult slip by. 'Do they still hang people here in 1967?' she asked Helena.

'It may cost me a very expensive holiday hideaway,' Xandra continued, flipping open a plastic box built into her desk revealing a pair of buttons, one blue and one vivid scarlet, 'but when I press this delightful red button, we will have one minute till this glorious old schloss explodes – with all your soldiers in it.' She was insanely excited by the prospect.

'And you as well,' Helena said.

'You disappoint me,' Xandra said almost petulantly. 'There is a reason my office is near the bottom of the building.'

Helena saw her meaning. 'Some kind of escape?'

'A very comfortable one,' Xandra confirmed. 'At the touch of the blue control.'

'That's disappointing,' Andy said sourly.

Gunfire from somewhere outside pushed Xandra and her goons to aim their weapons more accurately at their prisoners.

Helena glanced backwards at the mountains in the distance and the piste beneath them. 'Still, it's a hell of a view to die with.'

'Any last words?' Andy asked. 'Make them poignant and moving. You know I'm a sucker for that kind of thing.'

A familiar male voice came from the doorway. 'Well, I'd say you're not the only suckers.'

Two shots came from that door and Xandra Caprice's bodyguards dropped to the floor.

John Mason stood framed in the doorway, a pistol aimed at Xandra.

'John Mason,' Xandra's mouth opened in surprise. 'I thought you died. I paid that blonde a bonus for killing you.'

'She lied,' Helena said, still aiming her own rifle at Helena. 'She ripped you off. We told her he would survive, though I believe he did die on the operating table and they revived him. I saw it in his notes.'

'But we have a rule in the service,' Mason said coldly. '*Never die twice.*'

Andy indicated for Xandra to step back. 'Now be a good nutter and take your hand away from that button.'

'It seems you have the better of me.' Xandra looked from Mason at the door to Andy and Helena at the huge window, apparently in defeat. 'And you mean this button?' He brought her hand down on both red and blue buttons.

The first small explosion came almost immediately from below them.

'Oh, hell,' Helena said. 'Sixty seconds till this place goes up.'

Mason was already speaking on his radio. 'Evacuate. Everyone evacuate.'

Xandra laughed and dropped her pistol. 'You don't have time to get out of here.'

'*We* do,' Helena said before looking seriously at Mason. 'You're in trouble.'

'Unless he takes her escape route,' Andy suggested. She took a few steps to her right. By Xandra's side was a gap in the floor. The edges were clean and regular. 'And I'd say that's it there.'

Xandra made a move to sit in the leather chair behind the desk but Mason had moved closer and grabbed her arm.

Xandra cursed at them. 'No, it's…'

A larger explosion shook the building. They all staggered and caught at the walls to stay upright. Another explosion dropped Andy to one knee.

Xandra was hit worse. One of the statues, a bronze of a man standing so imperiously, was shaken from its plinth, knocking Xandra to the floor and then landing across her legs.

She screamed in agony.

Mason tried to lift the statue. 'Help me get her free.'

The huge bronze refused to move.

Helena and Andy both joined the effort to lift the statue but without success.

'There's no way we're moving that,' Andy said.

'Help me,' Xandra shrieked. 'I will kill you all.'

'That's hardly incentive to help you,' Helena said sourly.

'Offer him a bit of rumpo,' Andy said to Xandra while nodding towards Mason. 'He's shallow. He'd go for it.'

Mason shook his head firmly. 'I don't think so.' He tapped his watch. 'Forty five seconds. Come on. We need to go.'

'You can't leave me to die!' Xandra shrieked.

'Wanna bet?' Helena answered. She spoke to Mason. 'We've got our own way out. On your way.'

'If you insist.' Mason sat in Xandra's chair and looked around for some kind of control. 'Must be here...' He found a single control on the underside of the armrest and pressed it. The gap in the floor opened wider and the chair slid towards it. It began to disappear downwards. 'Thanks for the ride,' he called to Xandra.

Another blast shook the schloss and they heard masonry falling.

'Shall we go?' Andy suggested.

Helena raised the hand sporting her travel ring. 'Be a genuine pleasure.'

As they reached for their travel rings a whirlpool of energy opened up in the middle of the office.

That's enough,' a familiar and thoroughly annoying old voice said. 'you've succeeded. Best to leave this way.'

Xandra stared at the vortex in disbelief. 'What the hell is that?'

'Buggered if we know,' Andy answered.

She grinned at Helena and they both leaped into the energy whirlpool.

Helena and Andy leaped through a cinema screen and almost wound up sitting in the front row. Looking a few rows further back they saw three familiar faces.

'What the hell is going on?' Helena demanded, straightening up and starting to climb the stairs towards the three sitting comfortably in their seats. Andy followed close behind her.

'Ssh.' The old pharaoh held a finger to his lips. 'It's not finished.'

On screen, Xandra Caprice screamed obscenities as more explosions ripped her schloss apart.

'Damn shame all that art is going up in smoke,' Adam said.

'True,' the old man agreed. 'That's a completely unknown Van Gogh, you know.'

'Yeah?' Adam looked even more disappointed. 'Mum's favourite artist.'

Erimem leaned forward and looked across at Adam. 'Really?'

He nodded in reply. 'Yep.'

'Keep the portal open!' Erimem yelled. And then she was on her feet and sprinting towards the screen.

Adam's eyes widened in shock as he realised what she was about to do. 'Erimem!'

Andy reached to grab her friend, but she was too slow. 'What are you doing, you maniac?'

Erimem ran towards the screen and threw herself at the portal. A second later she was landing in Xandra Caprice's mountain-top retreat, standing over the fallen Principessa.

Xandra looked up at her and snarled. She tried to free herself and flailed for her fallen snake necklace, but Erimem kicked it away. 'I would love to stay and humiliate you a little longer but this place will explode in fifteen seconds and my mother-in-law is waiting for me.'

She ran to the wall and plucked the Van Gogh from it before running back toward the portal. On the way she swept up a first edition set of Pride and Prejudice from a display stand. A few more steps and Erimem leaped back through the portal.

The roar of another explosion filled the air and part of the floor cracked and fell away. The statue on Xandra's legs moved, tilted and then fell through the hole. She scrambled painfully to her feet.

Xandra saw only one escape She threw herself towards the portal but as her hand flailed for it, the opening shrank abruptly and closed.

Xandra screamed.

The largest of the charges detonated around the schloss and the top of the mountain exploded.

John Mason looked back from a sort of fully enclosed powered sleigh, which slid at speed away down the hill. He was pleased to see the helicopters had taken to the air before the schloss exploded, and just hoped the two women had escaped before the mountain had gone up.

* * * * *

In the cinema, a number of things happened at once. On screen the mountain exploded, Erimem leaped through the portal and just behind Erimem, as the portal closed, Xandra Caprice's manicured hand pushed through – and was then cut off as the opening closed violently.

The hand dropped to the carpet. It twitched once and then was still.

'That's put me off my popcorn,' the old pharaoh grumbled.

Andy couldn't resist the temptation. 'She won't have a hand in any more villainy.'

Helena just winced. 'Ouch.' She looked towards Erimem's grandfather. 'What about Mason?'

It was Adam who answered. 'He's doing fine.'

On screen, Mason was entering a mountain hotel where an attractive young woman was waiting.

'You're safe,' she said. Somehow she managed to make those two words sound like an invitation to her room. Or perhaps that was just how Erimem's grandfather wanted them to hear it.

Mason was looking very happy with his lot in life. He slid an arm round the woman's waist. 'Job done. Now... we might still make dinner if we hurry.'

Helena shrugged. 'Good luck to him. Maybe we should nip through and give them some protection, though?'

But Andy had already turned her own attention to Erimem's grandfather. 'So, is this all finished and done now?'

'Yes,' the old man said happily. 'You did very well. In fact, you've all done very well.'

'*Are You Being Served?*' Andy said.

Erimem shook her head in confusion. 'I don't understand.'

'TV reference,' Adam explained. '1970s comedy.'

'Oh.' Erimem noted that alongside the countless other useless pieces of trivia she had learned about her new home. 'But we are finished here?' she asked her grandfather.

'Oh, yes.' The old fellow had another drink. 'History is where it should be, so you can all go back to where you should be.'

That seemed to please everyone.

'Before we go, these are for you.' Erimem handed the three volumes of a first edition of *Pride and Prejudice* to Andy.

Andy's mouth dropped open and then broadened into a huge smile. 'Oh, wow. Thank you.'

'For giving me good advice.'

'I try.'

The cinema was already fading around them all.

Andy managed to shout 'See you later!' before the cinema and everyone in it disappeared.

Rene LeVal – or Phillipe Pascal if his newly obtained and freshly forged passport was to be believed – stepped from his plane into the blazing heat of the Caribbean.

After days of constant movement and terror that his past might catch up with him, Rene was finally able to relax. He had made it.

He had spent a day in a hospital bed recovering from whatever drug the lunatic woman Xandra Caprice had blown into his face. The memories of feeling and seeing his flesh burn would stay with Rene for a very long time and he doubted that he would ever be able to forget the acrid stench of his own charring skin even though it had only ever been in his mind.

Rene has slipped out of the hospital, returning to his hotel, picking up his passport and then heading to the airport. There had been plenty of police activity and Rene had wondered if the mixture of cash and precious stones in the false bottom of his suitcase might be discovered but he had checked in and boarded the plane without any trouble.

The flight itself had been rather dull, and Rene had taken the time to work out his plans for his new life. Even without the fortune he was sure Xandra Caprice had cheated him out of, he had enough to live a good life. He would buy a small house in a quiet neighbourhood in a small town and place the rest of his money securely in a bank. No, he would split it between two or three banks, just in case. He would take a mistress from the local European immigrant community, ideally a bored, married housewife. If she had a lot to lose, she would be unlikely to be looking for anything except some fun to pass the time while her husband was at work.

Good weather, good food, good sex… that was the life Rene dreamed of during the flight.

After collecting his suitcases, Rene wondered how long he would have to stay in a hotel until he could take ownership of a house.

'Taxi, sir?'

Rene had been so lost in his thoughts he hadn't noticed the attractive woman slide up to his side. He had never met a young, female taxi driver before but she was pretty, her eyes sparkled and there was a hint of amusement in her mouth.

'Why not?' Rene answered.

He declined the driver's offer to carry his cases. That was less chivalry and more of an unwillingness to let anyone else handle his money.

At the taxi, the driver opened the boot and Rene carefully put his cases inside. It was only when he closed the boot that he realised the driver was already in the car. As he reached for the door, the car pulled away and she waved at him cheerily.

Rene took two steps to begin running after the taxi when each of his arms was caught by a pair of powerful hands. Those hands were attached to strong looking men in cheap suits. They couldn't have been more obviously police if they had tattooed the word on their foreheads.

A third man joined them. He was older, had a moustache and a far more dangerous look to him. 'Rene LeVal,' he said in a gruff voice, 'we believe you know rather a lot about some criminal activities in Europe. Particularly a Mr Fournee in Belgium. Interpol suggested we let you land here before we get you to help us with our enquiries.' He smiled humourlessly. 'Safer for you and better for our sun tans.'

Every hint of hope and optimism abandoned Rene. He had come all this way and risked everything… and all to just wind up in prison.

Rene's shoulders slumped in defeat. He raised his hands so that he could be handcuffed.

'No need for that,' the gruff man said. 'If you're helpful enough, we might even see our way to returning your luggage and its... shall we say "contents"?'

Rene perked up at the sound of that. 'What do I need to do?'

'Tell us absolutely everything you know,' the moustached man said. 'Help us put Fournee and his partners away and we might even forget ever meeting you.'

Rene's mind raced. Putting Fournee in jail would reduce the chance of somebody coming after him... and the authorities might return his money...

Perhaps there was some hope after all.

Andy and Helena blinked back into existence in Erimem's habitat.

They both sighed enormously.

'Coffee?' Andy offered.

'Absolutely,' Helena agreed. 'If we hurry we'll catch the start of *Strictly*.'

Andy chuckled. 'Priorities, priorities...'

Erimem was about to say a goodbye to her grandfather in the cinema... but when she blinked, she and Admam were back in the doorway in Edinburgh. Somehow, they were back in the clothes they had been wearing when they left.

Adam looked around, relieved that everyone and everything was exactly as it had been before they had gone off to the Sixties. 'And we're back. I guess we've only been gone a few minutes.'

'Let's go to the pub,' Erimem said.

David and Fiona Docherty had barely taken their seats in *The Drouthy Duck* pub when Adam and Erimem came in. The young couple joined the older pair and sank into their seats with relief.

'You two been running?' Davd asked. 'You look knackered.'

'Long day,' Adam answered. '

'Bet you didn't sleep on the train,' his father answered. 'I've never been able to sleep on trains.'

'Piffle,' Fiona said. 'You can sleep anywhere.'

'I've gone right off trains,' Adam said. He grinned at Erimem. 'And planes. And submarines.'

'Submarines?' Davis looked at his son in surprise.

'He is joking,' Erimem explained quickly. She handed the painting she had rescued from Xandra Caprice's wall over to Fiona Docherty. 'I saw this. I did not have time to wrap it.'

Fiona looked at the painting. And looked. And looked. 'Oh,' she said finally. 'I mean... oh. It's beautiful. Thank you.' She put a pair of glasses on and peered closely at the canvas. 'Look at the paintwork. It's fabulous, thank you.'

'Adam said you like this artist,' Erimem said.

'I love Van Gogh,' Fiona agreed. 'If this was really by him it'd be worth millions. Whoever copied his style did a wonderful job.' She caught Erimem's hand and gave it a squeeze. 'You didn't have to do this, but thank you. Thank you so much.'

'It is my honour,' Erimem said pleased to see the gift so well received.

'Have you ordered?' Adam asked.

David scowled. 'Give's a chance. We just sat down.'

That told them how long they had been away. Not long at all. 'Fair enough,' Adam said.

A friendly server handed out menus to each of them. 'Menus for you.'

'Thank you.'

'Can I get you drinks while you decide on food?' the server asked, plucking a pad and pen from her pocket.

'Diet Coke,' Fiona said.

'Two of those,' David said miserably.

Adam glanced at Erimem. 'Something else for us?'

'Yes,' she answered firmly. 'We have earned a pint.'

ERIMEM

www.ingramcontent.com/pod-product-compliance
Lightning Source LLC
Chambersburg PA
CBHW061136200626
46817CB00016B/1658